Vices
&
Virtues

Kathryn Lamb lives quietly in Gillingham, Dorset, with her six children and five cats. Without the help of her family she would have found it a lot more difficult to write this book. She would like to thank them all, including some very special grandparents. Kathryn draws cartoons for *Private Eye* and *The Oldie*. She has written and illustrated a number of books for Piccadilly Press, which have been published in many languages throughout the world (including Italian, German, Dutch, Thai, Russian and Korean!). Her most recent book is *Love, Mates and Money*, the first title in the **Best Mates Forever** series.

Other titles by Kathryn Lamb:

The World According to Alex (Pick of the Year, Federation of Children's Book Groups Book of the Year Award – Longer Novel, 2000)

More of Everything According to Alex

The Last Word According to Alex

For Better or Worse According to Alex

Work, Rest and Play According to Alex

Summer, Sun and Stuff According to Alex

Honestly Mum!

Also in the BMF series:

Love, Mates and Money

bmf

Vices & Virtues

Kathryn Lamb

Piccadilly Press ● London

For Charlotte and Terry – and the little one.

First published in Great Britain in 2005
by Piccadilly Press Ltd,
5 Castle Road, London NW1 8PR
www.piccadillypress.co.uk

A catalogue record for this book is available from
the British Library

ISBN: 185340 807 7 (trade paperback)

1 3 5 7 9 10 8 6 4 2

Printed and bound in Great Britain by Bookmarque Ltd
Cover illustration by Kathryn Lamb. Cover design by Fielding Design
Text design by Textype Cambridge
Set in Soupbone, Regular Joe and Novarese

Papers used by Piccadilly Press are produced from forests grown and
managed as a renewable resource, and which conform to the
requirements of recognised forestry accreditation schemes.

walked up to Rob, who I've fancied for ages from a distance, at the end of biology today, and asked him for his number – and then gave him MINE! I asked the people he was with for their numbers *first* – and gave them mine – so it wouldn't look like I was singling him out, and I was ultra-casual, or as ultra-casual as it is possible to be when your voice comes out in a thin squeak . . . Rob and his friends were giving me funny looks, although they all gave me their numbers. Then I wandered casually away, tripping over a chair and then a school bag, before I made it out of the room – then I ran all the way to tell Sophie, who's in a different group, what I'd done!

'What did he say? What did he *say*?' Sophie is pleading. 'Aren't you glad now that I *made* you send him that text – you were so worried about being too full-on!'

I was worried about putting Rob off by coming on too strong. It took Sophie and me the whole of lunchtime break to decide what I should say. In the end we decided on: HI, ROB!

'Tash! What did he say?'

I flash my phone at Sophie. 'He said: HI, TASH!

Oh, Sofe – he's the BEST! Oh, I want to hug EVERYONE!'

'Aargh! You're squeezing me to death!' Sophie wheezes.

'I want you to be *pleeeased* for me!'

'I will be – if you let go! Phew! That's better – now I can breathe . . .'

'And you really *are* pleased for me?' I ask. I want her to share my happiness – we're Best Mates Forever, and we share *everything*!

'Of course I am! I am PUH-LEEASED!'

I look closely at Sophie – is that a glint of green in her blue eyes?

'You're not . . . jealous – are you?'

'Of course I'm not!' Sophie protests.

SOPHIE - GREEN-EYED MONSTER?

'It's just that you sounded a bit . . . um . . . and I don't want you to be jealous – I want you to be happy! Jealousy is a vice, isn't it?' I add, looking at Sophie enquiringly. Is she happy, or jealous – or both? She *is* a Gemini . . .

'I know, I know – according to you I'm vice on legs!' Sophie snaps.

'I never said that!' Why is she being so touchy?

'You didn't need to – you're right! I'm a chocolate-guzzling, money-hoarding beastwoman, who's going to be left on the shelf while you and Rob frolic on the beach and run hand-in-hand into the sea . . .'

'In the middle of October? Sofe, what are you on about? You will *never* be left on *any* shelf – believe me! I keep telling you – AGAIN AND AGAIN! – Rob's friend Luke really fancies you – it's sooooo obvious! He keeps looking at you!' This is true – and Sophie needs some serious cheering up.

'No, he doesn't! Luke NEVER looks at me.'

The cheering up isn't working . . .

'That's because every time you look in his direction, he looks away – I think he's shy. I'm sorry I didn't get his number today, but he wasn't with Rob when I went up to him. But I can easily get it – I'll text Rob now, and ask him for Luke's number. I'll have to explain why, or he'll think I'*m* after Luke!'

'Tash! N*o*!' Sophie grabs my arm, a look of alarm on her face.

'Why not?' I ask, surprised. 'You *do* still fancy him, don't you? You stayed up half the night last week telling me you did – remember?'

'Yes . . . but what if he hates me? I don't think I could cope with the pain of rejection now that you and Rob are practically an item – it would be too humiliating. We would become the one-with-a-boyfriend and the one-without-a-boyfriend.'

'Rob and I have texted "Hi!" to each other. I'm not sure if that makes us an item . . .'

Sophie turns soulful eyes on me, a look guaranteed to weaken the knees of any boy and send his testosterone levels rocketing. 'I think,' she says, 'I must prepare myself for the life of a nun.'

This comment instantly has me doubled-up, helpless with mirth. Sophie, meanwhile, is scribbling something in her sketchbook/diary.

'This is a list,' she says, holding it out to me, and waiting for me to stop writhing and be in a fit state to look at it. 'I've written down the things I need to do to turn myself into a Better Person. It'll give me something to think about to take my mind off the fact that you've got a boyfriend, and I haven't. And being a Better Person means that I won't mind so much that you've got a boyfriend, and I haven't.'

'You're mad,' I say, taking the diary, and reading:

How to Become a Better Person
(I really need to do this!)

1) Do and/or say something nice every day. For example: 'I am very pleased for you, Tash, because you have a boyfriend. I do not mind at all that I have no boyfriend. You must not let it bother you, the fact that you have a boyfriend, and I don't. You must remember that I don't mind. This is because I have a generous spirit.

2) Give to others. Give them support, advice, a shoulder to cry on, another shoulder to laugh on. Give them stuff.

3) Do not shout at/argue with parents, siblings, teachers, no matter how stupid, wrong or annoying they are. Smile at them instead! By doing this, I will indicate to them that I am on a higher level.

4) Stop obsessing about Luke. Unless he asks me out. Remember that there are other fish in the sea, although I do not want to go out with a fish. Even less do I wish to snog one.

5) Give up chocolate. Eat a healthy diet.

Signed:

Sophie Alice Edwards

I put down the diary.

'Well?' says Sophie, looking at me expectantly.

'You'll never keep to it,' I comment.

'I *will*! Watch me! I'm going to do something nice!'

I follow Sophie out onto the landing and to the door of the spare bedroom, which has become Mum's office. Sophie knocks. This is a mistake – Mum doesn't like to be disturbed when she's working, which is all the time.

'Yes? What?' Mum calls out in a weary, harassed voice.

Sophie pokes her head round the door and gives Mum a cheery smile. 'Would you like a cup of tea, Mrs Phillips? Or coffee? And a biscuit? You need to keep up your energy levels for all that work you're doing!'

'Er . . . what? Yes . . . OK . . . I'll have coffee – thanks! There are a few mugs in here which probably need to be taken away.'

I squeeze with Sophie into Mum's office, where all the available space is taken up by a filing cabinet, fax machine, photocopier, desk with computer monitor and a vast array of half-empty coffee mugs, several of which are going mouldy. No wonder I can never find any mugs downstairs – they're all in here!

Sophie gathers them up before I can help and looks like she's having trouble carrying too many coffee mugs at once – oh no! The worst has happened – she's dropped one – a coffee slick is streaming across Mum's desk, heading for the computer – the cordless mouse is drowning!

'GET ME A TOWEL FROM THE BATHROOM!' Mum yells. 'AND THEN . . . GO AWAY!'

'Are you sure you don't want me to get you Luke's number?' I ask a drooping Sophie, as we wander in the direction of her house. It would give me a good excuse to text Rob again! I WANT ANOTHER TEXT FROM HIM! It's been *hours* since the last one – has he gone off me? Has he met someone else?

'No . . . it's no good,' replies Sophie, sadly. 'I'm sure he hates me. Everyone hates me. Your mum hates me.'

'Oh, take no notice of her! She doesn't hate you! She's just stroppy and stressed because she works too much. She probably needs a man.'

Joking apart, I am concerned about Mum. She works all the time, and I sometimes feel like a nuisance, interrupting her hectic schedule with my occasional growing pains. I would like to be able to talk to her without feeling that I need to make an appointment . . . If she had a lurve life, would she be happier and less of a workaholic? Although I don't know how I'd cope with having a man around the place who wasn't Dad . . .

'And then I made everything worse by spilling coffee on her computer,' Sophie says with a sigh.

'Only on the mouse,' I point out. 'And you were trying to be nice – you didn't get much thanks.'

'I don't need thanks. Virtue is its own reward.'

'What does that mean?' I ask.

'It means that being a good person makes you feel good – the Feelgood Factor. Except that I'm not feeling very good.'

'I bet you'd feel good if Luke texted you, wouldn't you? And even better if he *snogged* you! Be *honest*! Honesty is a virtue!'

'Mmmmmmmm . . .' says Sophie, dreamily.

'I'll take that as a "yes"! Admit it, Sofe – you can't live without the Phwoar Factor, either!'

Chapter 2
Sophie

BRIGHT AUTUMN SUNSHINE has brought people out onto the playing fields during morning break at St Boris's Comprehensive. It has also brought out the wonderful chestnut highlights in Luke's glossy straight brown hair. He has an ultra-sexy floppy fringe and to-die-for long lashes over twinkly green eyes, and a cute lopsided smile – and I am goo.

LUKE

He is *not* looking at me – does he *ever*? I don't believe Tash when she says Luke fancies me. I think she's trying to cheer me up because *she's* the one who's on the verge of actually having a boyfriend! The boys who asked us out in Year Eight and then stood us up because they stayed at home to watch football on TV instead, and didn't bother telling us, don't count. Sadly, neither does Gareth, the hunk living next door to Mrs Ames, who Sophie and I lusted after when we were looking after the house and Mrs Ames's elderly mother while Mrs Ames was in Australia. Sadly it turned out that Gareth already had a girlfriend.

Three whole months have passed and we have all grown up a lot since then. Now we are in Year Ten, hanging out near the tennis courts with a group of other Year Tens, including Rob and Luke (sigh!), and keeping our distance from the Year Eight and Nine brats (including my delightful little brother, Kyle, who is now a TEENAGER – scaree!) who are collecting conkers under the towering horse-chestnut trees on the other side of the football field. Conkers! Why does EVERY-THING make me think of Luke? Conkers are the same colour as his hair, in case you're wondering.

I've had these feelings of unrequited lurve for Luke for ages – since the beginning of Year Nine, when he and Rob both joined the school and immediately became the Year Hunks, leaving a trail of sighing and yearning females wherever they went, although – frustratingly – they seemed more interested in riding their BMXes than they did in going out with girls, and were always talking about what they were going to do at the weekend or after school (on their bikes). Luke went out (briefly) with Jasmine Littlewood

JASMINE

– but there aren't many boys who *haven't* been out with Jasmine Littlewood (she is a babe; a boy magnet, although some of the girls call her worse names than that behind her long, slender back and cascade of spun-gold hair). Jasmine dumped Luke, saying that he was in love with his bike. I wanted to heal his wounds, and tell him that I could cope with a three-way relationship with him and his bike. But he didn't seem upset enough about the break-up of his relationship with Jasmine to need consolation. I have never found the courage to even say 'Hi!' to Luke, let alone tell him that I wish only to be his devoted lurve-slave until my dying day.

I haven't talked about my feelings for Luke to Tash *too* much (apart from when I stayed up half the night talking about them), because she is inclined to tease me – she knows that I blush like a sun-ripened tomato, which is really unfair and embarrassing! Tash, who never blushes, doesn't understand how awful it makes me feel. I tried explaining to her what it's like,

I BLUSH LIKE A SUN-RIPENED TOMATO

but she said that I shouldn't worry because it shows what a sweet person I am, with a caring, sensitive nature, which boys would find attractive. I don't believe her, and I'm worried that she'll say something to make me blush in front of Luke.

I wish I had more confidence. I'm so small, and I have freckles, which make me look about six years old. I suppose I should be grateful that Mum and Dad didn't call me Dot! Tash does the cool and casual thing much better than I do, although *she* insists that I *can* be cool, and that I have heaps of cool potential (as yet unrealised!). She's in supercool mode now, leaning against the wire fence of the tennis courts, tilting her head back slightly and half

TASH IS IN
SUPERCOOL
MODE...

closing her eyes, apparently enjoying the warmth of the sun on her face (only I KNOW what she's REALLY enjoying – being just a few feet away from Rob!). I notice that she has plastered spot concealer cream all over her nose. It has made her nose darker than the rest of her face, but at least you can't see the spot.

Rob and Luke are chatting together, as usual. When the bell goes for the start of lessons, they wander past us. Rob grins shyly at Tash from behind a stray lock of blond hair, and says, 'Hi!'

'Hi, Rob!' Tash replies, in a flirty, little girly voice. I wish she wouldn't do this! It sounds stupid! Luke doesn't even LOOK at me! WHYYYYY?

'Did you hear that, Sofe?' Tash hisses at me excitedly, after the boys have gone. 'Did you *hear*? He said, "Hi!" And then I said, "Hi!"'

ROB

'I heard.' I reply. 'Wow – things are really hotting up between you two. First you text "Hi!" then you say "Hi!" Whatever next? Perhaps you'll both have the word "Hi!" tattooed on your backsides!'

'Sophie! You *said* you wouldn't be jealous!'

'I am NOT jealous!' I say, through gritted teeth. 'I am very VERY GENUINELY PLEASED for you. Luke didn't even look at me . . .'

'He's shy, Sofe! Look – there's only one way to sort this out. Let's get texting!'

'No! Not now, anyway. Our phones will be confiscated. Let me think about it – maybe later.'

I am torn between wanting to know what Tash and Rob are texting to each other, and finding the full-on flirting a little hard to take while I am doing my wilting wallflower act – fate should not have cast me in this role! It is a mistake. Blondes are meant to have more fun! So why is Tash having more fun than I am? Does she *really* like Rob? Or does she just want to flirt and have a boyfriend so she can fit in with the other girls in Year Ten? I am not like that. I am SERIOUS about Luke . . . and I am NOT jealous! Or maybe . . . just the tiniest bit . . .

Tash isn't in my geography group – but Rob and Luke *are*. They *always* sit together – but today is different . . .

'Rob's gone to the dentist, sir,' I hear Luke tell Mr Sharpsand.

'OK, Luke. Thank you for telling me. Go and sit down, would you?'

Some other people have sat where Rob and Luke usually sit, and there are only two spare seats, one of which is . . . next to me!

MR SHARPSAND

Using powerful thought-waves, I attempt to draw Luke in my direction: Sit . . . next . . . to . . . me . . . sit . . . next . . . to . . . me . . . ohmigod . . . he . . . *is . . . sitting . . . next . . . to . . . me* . . .

SIT NEXT TO ME.....

POWERFUL THOUGHT-WAVES...

ohmigod . . . ohmigod . . . I . . . must . . . keep . . . calm . . . But what if I can't control myself? What if I suddenly leap on him and snog his face off – in the middle of geography? It could happen!

He *still* hasn't looked at me. Is he shy? Or am I hideous? He is concentrating on getting his books ready for the lesson. Summoning up all my courage, I attempt to say 'Hi!' but 'H–!' is all that comes out. I have lost the power of speech. I don't know how people write love poetry – true love is incoherent . . .

My stomach has turned into the most extreme roller coaster ride – I hope I'm not going to throw up! I need to focus. Mr Sharpsand is droning on about wetlands and water-tables and rising ocean levels and rivers and . . . I need the loo!

Then Luke looks at me – the briefest of glances! And now I wish he hadn't – because, in that briefest and potentially most significant of all moments, I *blew it* – well and truly! How do I know I blew it? Because I *smiled* at him! And it was not a normal smile. It was *not* one of the slow and seductive smiles which I have spent so many hours practising in the bathroom mirror – rehearsing for the one true moment of exquisite romance, that brief encounter between two people destined to

THE SMILE FROM HELL

be together . . . WHAT WAS IT ALL FOR?! No – this smile was the Smile From Hell. My jaw locked and my lips curled back to reveal firmly clenched teeth. No wonder he looked away quickly – no boy in his right mind would want to look at a mouth like that, let alone *snog* it! Not that he'd stand much chance of getting past those firmly clenched teeth . . .

I am burning up. My face is hot enough to melt a glacier – I am Global Warming Woman – and I *know* that my face has gone into full tomato mode. I want to cry. I wish Mr Sharpsand would say something that would give me an excuse for crying – but geography has never been the most emotionally charged lesson.

Instead, Mr Sharpsand says: 'I think congratulations are due to Sophie Edwards for a superb dam project – one of the best I've seen! A round of applause for Sophie, please!'

There is a polite but resentful ripple of applause from people who thought their dam projects were better. Everyone is looking at me – I can't bear it! I stare fixedly at the book open on the desk in front of me. I *hate* Mr Sharpsand!

'Are you OK, Sophie?' Mr Sharpsand enquires.

No, but I might be, if you'd leave me alone! I think.

'I'm fine. Thank you,' I say through gritted – as opposed to firmly clenched – teeth. I am struggling to keep my Resolution to Be Nice to Parents, Siblings and Teachers.

The remaining minutes of the lesson plod by – I wish I was invisible. At last the bell goes, and I pack my books away, trying not to think about the Smile From Hell, and how I blew any chance I ever had of making Luke fall in love with me.

'You've got a lovely smile, you know!' says a voice.

Looking up quickly, I see Luke looking at me, and he is . . . blushing!

'I've got to go,' he mutters, grabbing his bag and rushing out of the room.

I am speechless.

At lunchtime I tell Tash what happened – even though I am not sure what happened! I am quite confused, although I *think* Luke likes me! Tash says that it's been obvious from Day One that Luke likes me, and that the Luke Situation is driving her round the bend, and she's coming round to my house later to get things properly sorted out . . .

I am in the kitchen helping Mum (who only works a half day at the library on Wednesdays) unload the dish-washer and put plates away while I wait for Tash. She said there was something she had to go and do.

Mum is looking at me curiously. 'Judging by the dead-fish eyes,' she says, 'it's either love or you're going down with glandular fever. Which is it?'

'Love,' I whisper.

'Oh, I see. Do I know him?'

'I doubt it.'

'How old is he?'

'He's in my year.'

'What's his name?'

'Luke . . . Can I go now?'

But my escape route from the kitchen and Mum's intensive questioning is blocked by Kyle, who is standing in my way and refusing to let me get past.

'Get out of the way, Kyle!'

'Not till you tell me who your boyfriend is!'

'I don't have a boyfriend!'

'I heard you talking just now – so you can't deny it! You said his name was Luke . . . not . . . not . . . Luke Norris!'

'What if it is? What's it to you?'

Kyle gives a low whistle. 'Luke Norris is going out with *my* sister! How cool is that?' Kyle looks at me with a strange kind of respect. I can't remember him respecting me for anything until this moment! 'Luke Norris is only *the* most talented BMXer in the *entire* school!' he exclaims, in awed tones, standing aside at last to let me pass.

'And is he a nice boy?' Mum asks, anxiously.

'Oh, he's OK!' says Kyle. 'He's got the odd criminal conviction – nothing serious. I think he dabbles in drugs, gets involved in a bit of gangster warfare – but

always hands his homework in on time.'

'Oh, SHUT UP, KYLE!' I yell at him, just as Dad, who is home from the school where he teaches, walks into the kitchen.

'Anything I should know about?' he asks.

'No, Dad,' I reply. 'There's nothing you should know about, apart from the fact that Kyle is an idiot. And I wish everyone would leave me alone.'

I depart upstairs to my room, munching an apple as a concession to the 'Eat a Healthy Diet' resolution and to make up for the three Mars bars which I

EAT A HEALTHY DIET!

ate earlier. I am aware that I am not keeping my Resolution to Be Nice to Parents, Siblings and Teachers. I will try harder . . . I will smile at Kyle . . .

Soon, my thoughts give way to others. I have a

21

lovely smile – that's what Luke said . . . my insides melt at the memory! It wasn't the Smile From Hell, after all! Luke's lopsided grin is heavenly . . . I have a tickly, whirly feeling . . . One of my other resolutions was not to obsess about Luke . . . so I won't . . . I will not obsess about Luke . . . I will not obsess about Luke . . . I will not obsess about Luke . . . Luke . . . Luke . . . Luke . . .

Chapter 3

Natasha

I APOLOGISED TO Sophie again this morning, as we walked to school – having texted her last night – for not making it round to her house yesterday, but Things Got In My Way.

The first Thing was Kezia, my beloved big sister, who accused me of taking two boxes of henna hair dye from her room – *as if* I would do such a thing! Recently she has started dyeing her hair red, probably so that she and Carrot Boy, also known as Geoffrey the Boyfriend, can have matching hair – they are such a sweet couple! We had an argu-

I DIDN'T TAKE YOUR HAIR DYE – HONEST!

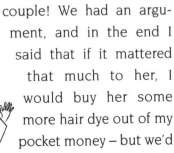

ment, and in the end I said that if it mattered that much to her, I would buy her some more hair dye out of my pocket money – but we'd have to rush before the shops closed. So she drove us into Bodmington where we bought hair dye, strawberry-flavoured lip gloss and a packet of extra-strong mints. I want to be properly prepared in case Rob decides to snog me.

We were just about to head for home when we bumped into Carrot Boy himself, wearing his favourite orange shirt and green jeans. The result of this chance encounter was that we all had to go and sit in a café and drink latte, which took ages (and it was revolting, although I pretended to like it because Geoffrey was paying).

WE HAD TO SIT IN A CAFÉ AND DRINK LATTE ...

When we eventually got home Mum was in a foul mood because she'd just incinerated the microwave pizza that she was going to give us for tea – and she took out her foul mood on *me*, saying that I would never pass my GCSEs unless I spent AT LEAST three hours a night doing my homework and coursework. Just because *she's* a workaholic, she expects everyone else to be one, too!

So I told her she ought to get out more. This didn't go down very well, and she shouted at me that chance would be a fine thing as she didn't have anywhere to go and she didn't have anyone to go with. She looked upset, and I felt bad for hurting her feelings. I found myself thinking of Sophie's resolutions to be nice, so I asked, tentatively, because Mum and I don't usually talk about the divorce, if she was upset about Dad and Wendy and the baby. She said that it was nothing for me to worry about (which meant 'yes'), and that doing lots of work helped her not to think about it. Then she added, rather wistfully, that it would probably be nice to get out occasionally – but that it would have to be with the Right Person. Then she switched back into normal mum mode and sent me upstairs to get on with my homework.

Upstairs in my room, getting on with my homework (not), I found myself thinking about Mum and how I could help her to find Mr Right. I remembered seeing her newspaper open on the Lonely Hearts page. It was opposite the page on which Mum was doing the crossword . . . but maybe Mum sees herself as a Lonely Heart! I tried hard to think of men we knew who might be able to cheer her up (less dodgy than meeting strange men through Lonely Hearts ads in newspapers!). I could only think of the plumber. He has been doing a lot of work at our house recently, and I noticed – when I handed him a cup of coffee – that he wasn't wearing a wedding ring. But the conversation between him and Mum has never progressed beyond the 'I think you'll find the whole cistern needs replacing, Mrs Phillips' level – and then I thought that he probably wasn't Mum's type, anyway. And then a little voice inside me started bleating that I didn't want Mum to have another man in her life because I wanted everything to stay the same. I've had enough massive upheaval to deal with because of the divorce! And then I felt disloyal to Dad for even thinking of replacing him with a plumber.

By now my head was seriously beginning to hurt, so I stopped thinking and gazed instead at those special messages stored forever on my phone and engraved on my heart: 'HI, TASH!' and 'HI!' and 'WHAT DO WE HAVE TO DO FOR BIOLOGY 2MORROW?' (I am in the same group as Rob for biology.) I texted him back: 'READ PAGES 116-134 OF

BASIC BIOLOGY AND WRITE ESSAY ON LIFE CYCLE OF MOTH. HOW R YR TEETH?'

But I didn't get a reply, which was worrying. Did I say the wrong thing?

'So that's why I couldn't come round to your house yesterday, and why you'll have to come round to mine later,' I finish explaining to Sophie, having filled her in on the My Mum is a Lonely Heart Situation, just as the bell goes for the start of lessons, and we are caught up in a thick stream of pupils surging down the corridor . . .

I am waiting by the main gate for Sophie at the end of the day when Rob and Luke ride past on their BMXes (which they keep chained up in the bike sheds during school hours).

'Hi, Rob!' I call out.

'Hi, babe!' he calls back to me.

Babe! BABE!!! He called me 'babe!' Ohmigod-ohmigodohmigod He . . . called . . . me . . . BABE!!! I have just melted into a puddle on the pavement. Jasmine Littlewood glides past and gives me a pitying look – but I don't care!

I am still fizzing like a firework fuse when Sophie finds me.

'As I've said before – and I mean it – I'm pleased for

you,' she says. 'But perhaps you shouldn't read too much into one word.'

'Don't be such a killjoy!'

'I'm just sounding a note of caution,' says Sophie, seriously.

'OK, so what's up? Something is . . . something's eating you . . . I'm meant to be the one who does the note of caution thing – not you.'

'I'm just . . . confused.'

'That sounds more like you!' I say, jokingly.

'Thanks. But I just don't get it – Luke didn't look at me *once*, all through double drama.' (Luke is Macbeth in a school production, and Sophie is playing the part of the Second Witch in the same production).

'So? It's not *Romeo and Juliet*, is it? Macbeth isn't *meant* to start eyeing up the Witches . . .'

'But even *after* the lesson – when I said, "Hi, Luke!" – he totally ignored me! I don't understand – what's his problem? Was it because the rest of the class was teasing me and the other witches, calling us the Weird Sisters? Does he think I'm weird?'

I sigh deeply. 'I told you – he's shy. Look, let's go up to my room and get your life sorted . . .'

'I TOLD YOU – HE'S SHY...'

'It's time for you and me to get down to some serious texting!' I tell Sophie firmly, enjoying the feeling that I have the Upper Hand, for once. It is usually the other way round, with Sophie the Soothsayer predicting my future and planning my life for me according to my stars, and getting me into situations . . .

Sophie nods uncertainly. 'I read my horoscope in *TeenScene* magazine,' she says. 'It said, "Expect the unexpected".'

'That's impossible. Forget horoscopes! Believe me – your future's looking bright! Now – I'm going to start by texting Rob.'

T2R: HI, ROB! CAN I HAVE LUKE'S NUMBER? IT'S FOR A FRIEND.
R2T: HI BABE!

YESSS!!! I am practically frothing – now I can *show* people that Rob thinks I am a BABE! This is another text to keep FOREVER!

R2T (continued): S CAN HAVE L'S NUMBER, NO PROBLEM. HE FANCIES THE PANTS OFF HER, BY THE WAY. U AND ME ARE JUST GO-BETWEENS.

'Nooo . . . that can't be right. We are *more* than just Go-betweens, surely? SOPHIE! Stop bouncing on the bed

like a kangaroo on a caffeine trip! It's mega-ANNOYING!
I KNOW he said he fancies the pants off you, but it's just
a figure of speech, it doesn't mean . . .'

R2T (again): HI. ME AGAIN. THIS IS L'S NUMBER. HE IS V V
CROSS ABOUT THE LAST TEXT. SAID I MADE HIM
SOUND LIKE A SLEAZE. SAID 2 TELL S HE IS NOT A
SLEAZE. SAYS HE WANTS TO B JUST GOOD FRIENDS
THEN C HOW IT GOES. TOLD HIM 2 SEND HIS OWN
TXTS. TXT BACK S'S NUMBER.

I feel like a deflated balloon. So does Sophie, judging
by the expression on her face.

'There's nothing wrong with Just Good Friends,' I say
to her. 'It's better than being Go-betweens.'

'The JGFs and the GBs.'

'That's us.'

'It's a start . . .' says Sophie, re-inflating slightly.

'Definitely!' I agree. I am *not* going to let my chance
of acquiring a drop-dead-gorgeous boyfriend with a
bum-to-die-for slip away. I always assumed, for some
reason – probably because she is blonde and bubbly
with legs up to her armpits – that Sophie would be the
first to have a proper boyfriend, and I would be left
waiting for Mr Right, or even Mr Will-Have-to-Do . . .
and I wasn't sure how I was going to cope with this. But
now Fate has intervened, and our Fate Mates have
come bar-spinning into our lives on their BMXes at

exactly the same moment . . . so it is time to seize the opportunity and to take control of our destiny.

'We have to knock their socks off!' I exclaim. 'And I've got just the thing to do it!' I reach under the bed and produce two boxes of 'Flaming Red' hair dye from the 2Dye4 range of hair products.

'Red!' I announce. 'The colour of passion! It's obviously working for Kezia – so why not for us? When Rob and Luke see our hair, they'll be amazed, they'll be dazzled, hypnotised like rabbits caught in the headlights, and we can just reel them in!'

'Do you reel rabbits in?' Sophie looks uncertain.

'Why are you looking at me like that? I thought this would be just your style – wild and impulsive and . . .'

'Red.'

'Yes! Oh, come on, Sofe! It's about time we did something fun together, like dyeing our hair! We need to make an impression.'

'Yes – but it's got to be the RIGHT impression! I don't want to frighten Luke. I've just sent him my number and a text to say "Hi!" and he hasn't even replied. I'm getting really nervous now, Tash! Can you text Rob and find out why? Oh, pleeease? Pretty please? Be a nice little Go-between!'

I pull a face at Sophie and grab my phone. I really want to get this sorted out – I want Sophie to be happy . . . I want us *both* to be happy! Happy and IN LURVE . . .

I want a total First Boyfriend and First Kiss scenario!

T2R: WHY NO REPLY TO S FROM L?
A few minutes later . . .
R2T: L IS A SHY GUY. XXX

He sent me KISSES! I am more than a Go-between! I am fizzing again.

'I don't get it,' says Sophie. 'He's so good at acting – how can he be shy?'

'A lot of actors are – they only stop being shy when they go on stage.'

'He can't be *that* shy. He went out with Jasmine Littlewood – and survived!'

Sophie's phone be-beeps, and we bump heads in our haste to read the message – it is from Luke:

'WANT TO C A FILM? U, ME, R AND T? MEET AT THE CINEPLEX 2MORROW 8.30 PM? R'S IDEA – GOT ME 2 TXT U COS HE'S OUT OF CREDIT.'

Sophie and I hug each other – our First Date! Sophie wants to text back, 'YESSSSS!!!' – but I tell her that 'OK' will do. 'I'm sure he's only saying it was Rob's idea because he's shy!' Sophie exclaims. 'Oh, Tash – shy guys are so *cute* – don't you agree? He must *really* like me to go on a date with me! He's overcome his shyness – for ME!!! Oh, Tash – you were right! He DOES like me!'

We both agree that the best thing of all is that it is a

Double Date, which means that no one gets left on the shelf, and we can go on being Best Mates Forever WITH BOYFRIENDS!

We decide to celebrate by dyeing our hair.

The results are stunning. My hair has a reddish-auburn glow – I really like it! It is a Whole New Me, a Wild and Unconventional Me, a Take-Me-Rob-I'm-All-Yours Me!

Sophie's hair is –

'Flaming ginger!' she moans, running her bright orange fingers through her hair in despair – she is in Major Crisis Mode. The gloves that were provided with each kit to protect our hands got holes in them after we over-inflated them and turned them into cows' udders.

'Stop staring at me like that, Tash!' Sophie exclaims. 'Haven't you ever seen someone with mad orange hair before? Perhaps I could join a circus and become a clown with a red nose, huge shoes and a pair of baggy old trousers held up with braces! Luke's going to run a mile! He won't want to be Just Good Friends any more – it'll be more like Just Forget It! Oh, this is a TOTAL NIGHTMARE!' she wails. 'Why did I let you persuade me to dye my hair?'

'I . . . I thought it would be fun. I thought your hair would go auburn like mine . . . but . . . but . . . I suppose it's because you're blonde . . .' I feel so helpless – I don't know what to do or say!

'It *will* wash out, won't it?' Sophie asks, desperately. 'Tell me it *will* wash out!'

'Eventually . . . Listen, Sofe. It's not that bad – really! Ginger's OK. Think about Mitch from the Melodics – he's ginger and he's cool!'

'But blondes have more fun!' Sophie wails. 'When did you last hear anyone say: "Ginger-haired people have more fun!"?'

She is on the verge of tears. I feel bad – this is all my fault. I am saved from having to say anything by Kezia hammering on the door and demanding to know what we've been doing in the bathroom all this time. 'Dad's on the phone, Tash, and he wants to talk to you – so HURRY!' she yells.

I emerge gingerly – although Sophie does 'gingerly' better than me at the moment, ha ha – from the bathroom and am confronted by Kezia, hands on hips, face like thunder.

'I thought so!' she exclaims. 'You *did* take my 2Dye4 kits!'

'But I bought you some more!' I shout back, rushing past her and into Mum's room so that I can pick up the phone. I really look forward to Dad's phone calls. I hope this one is to arrange for me to go and visit him, as it is AGES – over a month! – since I last went.

'Why are you copying me, anyway?' Kezia demands, as Sophie slinks into the room and perches on the edge of the bed, twiddling her ginger hair and looking thoughtful. She is not crying – thank goodness!

'I'm *not* copying you!' I retort. 'Hi, Dad! No – nothing's wrong! I'm just shouting at Kezia – so things are pretty normal here, I guess . . .'

Dad wants me to go and stay with him for a few days over half-term. I call downstairs to Mum, who says that it's fine. I miss Dad, and I apologise again for having missed the last visit (they are meant to be fortnightly) because I was playing in a really important football match. Then I ask how everyone is at his end, and I ask if baby Alfie (my little half-brother) has done anything new since I last saw him.

I feel happy and sad after putting the phone down – sad because Dad is so far away, but happy because I'll be seeing him next week. I hope Mum's OK. I must give more thought to how to find her the Right Man. She deserves to be happy, so I must make an effort to over-come my fear of things changing. This is my own good resolution – to make Mum happy! An unconnected thought suddenly hits me: how am I going to survive being away from Rob for a few days next week, especially if we are going steady by then!

Sophie seems to have cheered up. 'I just remembered!' she says. 'Luke said I had a lovely smile! So it's my smile he likes – I don't think he's that bothered about my hair! I just need to keep smiling... I'll be brave. I'll smile through my tears!'

Mum comes into the room – she is not smiling. 'Dyeing your hair won't help you pass your GCSEs!' is her only comment.

Mum seriously needs to lighten up. I expect she's upset about Dad... I don't want my visits to make it hard for her... I WILL find her a man!

I am SOOOOOO looking forward to the Date tomorrow! I'll tell Mum about it when she's calmed down about the hair-dyeing. (We accidentally dyed parts of the bath mat and several towels red, and a portion of the loo seat too...) I hope Sophie's OK – her hair isn't that bad but she's such a Drama Queen – I think she's in lurve with lurve, rather than with Luke himself, although I'd *never* say that to her! I'm happy with my hair, although it will take some getting used to, and it's nearly half-term ... and I'll be seeing Dad soon... I have a tra-la-la feeling...

Chapter 4

Sophie

DOUBLE DATE DAY!!!

Things are looking good. Mum has recovered from the shock of seeing me with bright ginger hair, and has managed to get hold of her friend Veronica, who works at A Cut Above, the trendy new hair-salon above Froth's Coffeehouse in the mall. I am to go there straight after school today, and Veronica will see what she can do . . . (I have stuffed some clothes to change into at the bottom of my bag, as I am *not* going to wear my school uniform to the salon!)

But first I have to survive school. Mum refuses to write a note saying that I could not come to school because my hair turned ginger. She wouldn't even write a note to say that I was absent because of a bout of twenty-four-hour bubonic plague! So I have scraped my hair back into a tight bun, mostly concealed by a black scrunchie, and have covered my head in so many hair-slides that you can hardly see any hair. Dad says that he likes my new hairstyle, and I give him an 'OH, PUHLEEASE!' look. Unfortunately, we are not allowed to wear hats in school. I don't know why; perhaps they are worried that our brains will overheat. Kyle laughs at me as I leave the house, but I remember my Resolution to Be Nice to Parents, Siblings and Teachers, so I SMILE at him – which unnerves him.

I have my calming stone in my pocket and a copy of the *Teen Astrologer's Guide to Lurve* in my bag (this came free with the latest copy of *TeenScene* which I have also stuffed in my bag). The chart at the front of the astrologer's guide tells me what I already know: that I am Gemini with Aquarius rising and the Moon in Taurus. It also tells me that October is the ideal month to meet my Fate Mate (who

SCENE FROM SOPHIE'S SKETCHBOOK:

I AM GEMINI WITH AQUARIUS RISING AND THE
MOON IN TAURUS ...

JUPITER HAS JUST ENTERED THE SEVENTH HOUSE
OF VENUS!

should, ideally, be a fire sign, such as Leo), because
Jupiter has just entered the seventh house of Venus –
and it's all happening in the house of lurve! I wonder if
Luke is a fire sign – he's got to be! The way those fiery
chestnut highlights in his hair catch the sun ... I'm
melting again ...

The autumn sun behind us turns Tash's hair into a
blaze of fiery red and chestnut brown as we walk
through the main gate.

'It looks great, Tash,' I tell her. 'I'm hopefully getting
mine sorted out later, just in time for the Date!

The Date!!!' I cling to Tash's arm and squeeze it hard. I'm so excited I can hardly BREATHE! 'Come with me to that hair place, will you? They'd *better* sort it out for me – my entire future prospects of becoming the lurve of Luke's life depend on it! So, assuming my hair gets sorted and my life is saved, then we can go back to my house – or yours – and get ready! Did you know that Jupiter's entered the seventh house of Venus – isn't that brilliant? Do you think Luke's a fire sign? Do you think the fact that he asked us out means that he wants to be More Than Just Good Friends – that's MTJGF? Do you think he'll . . . he'll KISS me!!! Or will he hate me when he sees my hair? Mum's friend might make it WORSE! Maybe he'll dump me before we've even BEEN on the date! Then it will be just you and Rob – I don't think I could bear it! GIVE ME CHOCOLATE! LOTS OF CHOCOLATE!!!'

'SOPHIE! Calm down! Please! Take deep breaths!' Tash has taken me firmly by the shoulders and is looking into my eyes. 'That's right – exhale slowly now . . . Do that Zen breathing thing where you close one nostril.'

'Thanks, Tash – I'm OK now!' I say, feeling the smooth cold surface

NESTLING IN MY POCKET...

THE CALMING STONE,

A HALF-EATEN
BAR OF
CHOCOLATE,

THE
WRAPPER
FROM
ANOTHER
BAR...

of the calming stone, nestling in my pocket beside a half eaten bar of chocolate and the wrapper from another bar of chocolate which I shared with Tash yesterday . . . Oh, the shame of it! I have broken my Resolution *Not* to Eat Chocolate one and a half times – at least!

At morning break we are down the side of the tennis courts as usual with the other Year Tens, including Rob and Luke. Rob keeps breaking off from his conversation with Luke to wink at Tash, who does this silly, simpering thing, pursing her lips and fluttering her eyelashes. It is quite unTash-like, and I am beginning to find it annoying. I would never simper like that if Luke winked at me, which he hasn't . . . He hasn't even looked at me . . . which is probably just as well – I'd rather he looked at me *after* I've had my hair sorted out. Although he could at least *glance* in my direction.

'Oh, look! It's the Witches from *Macbeth*!' Jasmine Littlewood and her friend Jocasta are giggling and making it perfectly obvious that they are talking about *us*, as they wander past. (Apart from Jocasta, Jasmine doesn't have any friends – her sarcastic manner had alienated nealy all the girls in our year.)'*Love* the hair, Sophie!' Jasmine adds, sarcastically.

'Take no notice!' Tash hisses at me, glaring angrily at Jasmine and Jocasta. 'Those two airheads are the *real* witches!' (I am in the same drama group as Sophie but I failed the audition to be a witch – Sophie and two other girls were chosen – but Jasmine has been calling us 'the Witches' and 'Weird Sisters' ever since.)

To my extreme annoyance, Jasmine glides over to

POWER FLIRTING

Rob and Luke, Jocasta in her wake, and starts coming on to Luke in the most blatantly obvious way, all fluttering lashes and lip gloss. Tash could learn a thing or two about simpering from Jasmine – she is a true professional. This is full-on power flirting.

'Of all the . . .!' Tash explodes, before she is totally goldfished, and stands there, opening and closing her mouth.

'But . . . but she dumped him!' I wail, covering my mouth with my hand so that no one apart from Tash hears my cry of distress as we are standing a short distance from the rest of the Year Tens. 'What's she playing at! I know – I know what this is about! She *knows* that I like him – she's noticed me looking at him during *Macbeth* – so she's trying to get him back, just out of spite! She doesn't even *like* him!'

'That sounds like her,' says Tash, her eyes trained on Rob. I can see that she is willing him not to start chatting to Jasmine and Jocasta.

To our relief, Jasmine and Jocasta soon wander away again – Jasmine tosses her head, flicking her long blond hair back over her shoulder and giving Luke a little smile and wave as she glides away, wiggling her backside. She gives me a triumphant look as she passes by. HOW OBVIOUS?!

'See what I mean?' I whisper to Tash. 'This is *awful!*'

'Don't worry, honey!' Tash says, putting her arm round my shoulders. 'Luke's *got* to like you more than Jasmine – or he's an idiot! I'm SURE he was only smiling at her because she was making him nervous!' I'm SURE Tash is right – at least, I *think* I'm sure . . .

I feel *much* happier now – a hundred times happier! Mum's friend Veronica has put streaks of blond, brown and auburn in my hair and it looks amazing! She has cut it as well, and my hair now has STYLE – shorter at the back and longer at the front . . .

MY HAIR HAS STYLE!

'You look like a supermodel!'

Tash exclaims, as Veronica shows me the back of my head in a mirror. 'Wait till Luke sees you!'

Mum arrives at the salon to pay (they stayed open late especially for me). I give her a big hug and thank her and Veronica for saving my life. 'You have narrowly averted the worst hair disaster in the history of hair!' I tell them. Mum likes my hair, too – she says that I look older. YESSSS!!!

We go downstairs to Froth's Coffeehouse, which

FROTH'S
SPECIAL
HOT
CHOC ☆
WITH
WHIPPED
CREAM!

stays open late on Friday evenings, for a not-a-latte. I have hot chocolate instead, and Tash has a Diet Pepsi – she doesn't want to put on weight before the Date this evening! I know that one of my resolutions was to give up chocolate, but hot chocolate is a drink, so it doesn't count!

I tell Mum about the Date. She says 'Oh . . . I see . . .' and looks thoughtful and slightly worried. Then she switches into full intensive questioning mode, but doesn't seem happy with my answers:

1) What film are you going to see?	Don't know. The film is not as important as the company.
2) When will you be back?	After the film has ended.
3) When does the film end?	Don't know.
4) Why does it have to be such a late film?	The earlier ones are too early.
5) How will you get back?	We'll phone you for a lift but don't park where Rob and Luke can see you, and don't get out of the car. We'll find *you*. Please.
6) Do I know the boys' parents?	How should I know?
7) Don't be rude. I asked you a question.	I answered it.
8) I shall have to talk to your father about this.	For God's sake – if we don't get a move on we're going to miss this date altogether, and my whole life will be ruined!

I think someone put too much caffeine in Mum's latte! At last we make it back to the house with just an hour and a half to go until we meet the boys . . .

Tash dashes back to her house to tell her mum that

she's going out but everything's OK because Sophie's mum or dad will meet us after the film – and can she stay with me tonight?

Tash returns with her stuff. 'I've got to phone Mum when we get back to tell her I'm OK – otherwise every-thing's fine – and we're going on our first Double Date! Isn't it AMAZING! AND it's half-term! Kezia wants us to bring Rob and Luke to the house so she can check them out – I wouldn't mind showing him off to her! She seemed quite taken aback that I'd got a boyfriend. She ought to realise I'm catching up with her, and I'm soon going to overtake! She's probably expecting me to bring home some spotty nerd in an anorak – so it'll be a big surprise when I walk into the room arm-in-arm with the Incredible Hunk!'

'But going out with someone isn't all about impressing other people – you've got to actually *like* the person. Otherwise you're like Jasmine Littlewood,' I comment.

'I know that! What are you implying?'

'Nothing. But do you actually *like* Rob?'

'Of course I do! How *could* you say I'm like Jasmine Littlewood?' Tash exclaims, looking hurt and offended.

'I didn't say you were *like* her.'

'You did! And you're a fine one to talk – I think YOU are in lurve with lurve! Nothing to do with Luke.'

'What? That is *so* . . . not true!' How *could* she say something like that?! The atmosphere in my room

DEAD SEXY? MORE DEAD FISH, IF YOU ASK ME!

seems to have cooled suddenly. Tash needs to learn how to take constructive criticism, and stop lashing out with wild and obviously untrue remarks!

We get ready in silence. Tash is putting on so much lip gloss that her lips make a little unsticking noise when she opens her mouth, and she practises a really stupid pout in the mirror which makes her look like a fish but *she* obviously thinks it's dead sexy. More dead fish, if you ask me . . .

She looks around and glares at me, and I look away. That sparkly black strapless top is *so* last year! Why is she wearing it with *that* brown mini-skirt? Her legs are too short to look right in a mini-skirt. Those shoes are awful . . . I realise that I am *not* keeping my Resolution to Be Nice to Parents, Siblings and Teachers – Tash and I are so close that she counts as a sibling, although at the moment she is not my favourite sibling – but at least I am keeping my mean thoughts to myself, unlike Tash! How dare she say that I am in lurve with lurve, and not with Luke?! I love him TOTALLY!

Mum pokes her head round the door, and can't help smiling. 'You both look lovely!' she says. 'Sophie – you look sweet!'

As soon as she has gone I rip off the clothes I was wearing and find some alternative ones – as unsweet as possible! I think I look good in black – black top, black trousers, black shoes, black belt, matching black bag, black socks and black underwear. At least ONE of us doesn't look like they're on a TV programme called *What Not to Wear on Your First Date*!

I am getting serious butterflies now – I think there are Madagascan moon-moths in my stomach! I pick up *TeenScene* magazine and flick through it, stopping on a page with the arresting headline: 'Every girl about to kiss her boyfriend will need a phone like this!' The article is about the smell-phone, which has an 'electronic nose' which can detect bad breath! ('It pings if you pong!')

I wish I had a phone like that! My insides have just gone 'Wheeeeee!' down a water-slide at the thought of

Luke kissing me, and my knees feel strange. I check in my bag for my emergency mints, and apply some more Cherrypie and Kiwi lip gloss.

'Time to go!' Mum says, poking her head round the door. 'I'm running you down there, and Dad's going to pick you up later. Make sure you phone us as soon *as the film has finished* – we will be waiting for your call.'

'Yes, Mum – OK! And have you remembered about dropping us round the corner from the Cineplex, *not* right outside it?'

There is still an atmosphere between Tash and me when we meet the boys. We are both so nervous that we have been snapping at each other – I know this is stupid, but I feel on edge. What if Luke tries to kiss me? What if my teeth get in the way?! Rob seems to sense that we are not one hundred per cent chilled, and he keeps glancing at each of us nervously. Luke smiles his wonderful lopsided smile at me, and I am goo again. Supergoo! I am *sure* that Luke and I *must* be More Than Just Good Friends – he melts my insides!

'I like your hair,' he says.

I feel myself going full tomato . . . Oh *no*! The Smile From Hell is back – all curling lips and stuck-together teeth.

Luke wanders off and looks in the window of a near-by games shop.

'He really likes you, you know,' Rob says to me unexpectedly, making me jump, and then blush again. 'He wanted me to tell you. He's really shy.'

'Oh, that's so cute!' I exclaim.

Rob shrugs and looks awkward, for some reason. Tash shakes her head. I bet she thinks that Luke should tell me himself how he feels! But I don't care.

Rob buys us all Coke and popcorn in the foyer of the Cineplex while we wait for our film to be called. This is

what Dad usually does. I half expect Rob to ask if any of us needs the loo before we go in – I *do* – but I don't want to go in case the film starts and I can't find Luke again.

We sit in the back row. I've heard that this is traditional for those who are about to snog . . . and presumably for those who are about to receive their First Kiss!

I rummage in my bag for my emergency mints. I pop

several in my mouth – they are extremely strong and mix strangely with the Coke and popcorn. My eyes water.

'Don't cry!' says Luke. 'The film hasn't started yet!'

I get the giggles (more like nervous hysterics), and Coke and popcorn and bits of mint shoot out of my mouth and down the neck of the person sitting in front of me.

'Oh! I'm sooo sorry!' I bleat, as a girl from the year above me turns round and gives me an evil look. I shrink back in my seat.

I am uncomfortably aware that Rob is snogging Tash next to me. He has stopped behaving like my father! If this is her First Kiss – and she has led me to believe that it *was* during our regular late night SAYS (Spill All Your Secrets Sessions) she has very quickly got the hang of it! Surely the moment has arrived for *me* to get to work on *my* snogging skills?! Then I remember, Luke is shy . . . and so am I . . .

There is something resting on my knee. It is Luke's hand! Ohmigod. What NOW? I don't know what to do about the hand on knee situation! HELP!!! With a tremendous effort, because my neck has become rigid, I turn my head (creak . . . creak . . .) to look at Luke . . . he is looking at me . . . his lips are slightly parted . . . he leans towards me . . .

'Hi, Luke! GOTCHA!' The girl whose neck I spat popcorn down – I think her name is Lydia – has turned round in her seat and is grinning at Luke. Luke springs away from me, blushing. Even in the dark I can *feel* him blushing, just like I am, with embarrassment and disappointment in equal measure.

'I *thought* it was you!' Lydia continues. 'But my eyes only just got used to the dark!

She is completely ignoring my existence.

'It's *really* nice to see you Luke!'

I can't see her face very clearly but I can *hear* her eyelashes fluttering. Looking quickly at Luke I see that he is smiling – is it just because he's nervous, like Tash said?

The advertisements and trailers have finished and the film begins. Rob stops snogging Tash. I think they have both come up for air! The film features Matt Hoffman, a famous BMXing man, and most of the film is taken up with sequences of Matt Hoffman and others doing extreme stunts on their bikes in a variety of different locations and somehow managing to defeat a gang of unpleasant-looking aliens on bikes, thereby saving the world in a cool and casual manner. It is a stupid and *boring* film, but I don't want it to end because I want to go on sitting next to Luke!

I am *y-e-a-r-n-i-n-g* for him to kiss me or hold my hand. Can't he *feel* me yearning? I have never yearned like this before! But both boys seem to be mesmerised by the film. I am also yearning to go to the loo.

Summoning up all my courage (and driven by my

desperation to be kissed!) I lightly touch Luke's hand, which is resting on the arm of the seat – he takes my hands, leans over again . . . it MUST be First Kiss moment AT LAST!!!

Or not. Lydia twists round in her seat, giggles and blows a kiss to Luke, who springs away from me again! I don't really know Lydia, but I *hate* her! She's ruined everything!

By the time the end credits roll, Lydia has managed to ruin a further two potential First Kiss moments. Luke keeps smiling back at her – but I suppose he can't help being friendly and she must be making him *very* nervous! I content myself with aiming a look to kill at the back of her head whenever she *isn't* twisting round to flirt with Luke – which is nearly ALL of the time – I'm GLAD I spat popcorn down her neck.

We all get up to leave. I am confused – excited and tingly at the thought that Luke obviously *wanted* to kiss me – but upset and frustrated that he didn't just ignore the loathsome Lydia and find a moment when she *wasn't* looking round! I am also in desperate need of a loo.

Outside in the foyer Tash is wearing Rob like a new coat. I phoned Dad from the loo and asked him to come and get us – it was a relief to hear his voice. He sounded concerned, and said that I didn't sound very happy – was I all right? I said I was fine.

'Wasn't the film great?' Rob enthuses.

'Oh, yes!' Tash agrees, in her flirty, girly voice. I am certain that she hated the film as much as I did. Why does she have to put on an act for Rob's benefit? I want her to behave like she normally does – and talk in a normal voice.

'I really hope they make *Alien BMXers* 2!' Rob continues. 'By the way, Luke and I are going to be at the skate park tomorrow – would you girls like to come along? We might go bowling at the rink later, or something.'

'Oh, yes!' Tash says. Can't she say anything else?

Luke gives me a sideways look. 'Will you be there?' he asks.

Summoning hidden reserves of cool and casual which I never even knew I had, I take a deep breath and say: 'I might . . .'

'Good,' he says, and, leaning forward, he kisses me on the cheek.

I am rooted to the spot, delicious tingles shooting up and down my spine and round my body. I am on fire! OK – so it was just a kiss on the cheek – but it will do for now! Next time . . . who knows? Tongues?! AWESOME!!!

I am still quivering when a familiar voice says: 'Hello!'

Oh *no*! At the exact moment when my cool rating just zoomed into outer space, leaving Tash as a tiny speck far, far below – and Jupiter was aligned with Mars and having the best party in the house of lurve – along comes . . .

Dad.

Mum must have forgotten to tell him to park one street away from the Cineplex and *on no account to get out of the car!* NIGHTMARE! W*hy* do my parents want to ruin my life? First it was Lydia, now Dad: *everybody* wants to ruin my chances of being kissed properly for the first time! WHY???!!!? And it is far too soon to introduce Luke to Dad – poor Luke! Especially since he suffers from shyness – this must be really nerve-racking for him! But there is nothing I can do . . .

DAD IS WEARING A
BOTTLE-GREEN
ZIP-UP CARDIGAN

'Hello, everyone,' says Dad, who is wearing a bottle-green zip-up cardigan. 'Good film? Are you going to introduce me, Sophie?' He has fixed Rob and Luke with a protective father hard stare.

'Erm,thisismydad,' I mumble, staring at the ground and wishing it would swallow me up.

'And what are your names?' Dad demands of the boys in a voice which suggests that he is about to ask them for some form of ID. Rob and Tash quickly side-stepped apart as soon as Dad appeared.

'This is Rob, and this is Luke,' I say. 'I think we'd better go now, Dad.'

I hurry him away before he has a chance to ask the boys how old they are, or what their intentions are towards his only daughter, and her friend.

'Nice to meet you!' Dad calls back to them. 'Don't stay out too late! See you again – perhaps!'

'Dad!'

'Should I offer them a lift?' Dad enquires.

'No!'

'Really, Sophie! Anyone would think you were embarrassed by me!'

Our feud is forgotten – Tash and I are friends again. We have too much to talk about, whether it's one significant kiss on the cheek (me) or full-on snogging (Tash). After phoning her mum to say we're back safely, Tash manages to reassure me that Luke isn't going to dump me because I have a dad who wears a bottle-green zip-up cardigan. She also manages to reassure me that Lydia is not a threat to perfect happiness as she already has a boyfriend.

'Rob is the best snogger!' Tash says with a sigh (not

for the first time), as we lie in bed listening to the gentle tinkling of the windchimes and *Lament for Lost Souls*, the latest CD by my favourite band, the Melodics. 'Now I know that I was right – Rob DOES fancy me, and we are DEFINITELY More Than Just Good Friends and MUCH more than Go-betweens! And snogging has gone right to the top of my list of things I like to do! Mmmmm!'

And it's at the top of my list of things I'd *like* to do! 'Luke is . . . *mmmm* . . .!' I comment, not to be outdone. The memory of that kiss lingers on, even if it left *something* to be desired – or looked forward to – a *proper* kiss on the lips would be good, with or without tongues. I'm not *too* fussy!

My phone beeps! There is a message from Luke: 'C U 2MORROW. XXX.'

I place my phone on the pillow beside me. I can't stop smiling.

Turning to Tash to show her my message, I see that she is already asleep – all snogged out . . . Hasn't she ever heard of playing hard to get? Apparently not . . .

As far as I am concerned, one kiss equals total bliss! And one more would be *total phwoar*!!!

Chapter 5

Natasha

SOPHIE IS DRIVING ME MAD. She keeps going on (and *on*) about one kiss. Luke kissed her once – on the cheek. So? Rob is the best snogger – as I keep telling her. But she doesn't listen. She's totally obsessed.

I have had two messages from Rob: the first was to remind me to meet him at the skate park at midday (as if I'd forget); the second was to tell me that I am a RED-HOTSEXYBABE! But when I try to show this message (which is surely a declaration of undying lust) to Sophie, she doesn't seem interested. All she can talk about is a message that she has just received from Luke that says: 'HI!'

I have had enough. I tell Sophie that I am going back to my house to fetch some stuff. She doesn't react – just sits staring at her phone – and then I float down the stairs and out into the street, dreaming of Rob. I usually go to football practice with the Southway All

Girls' Football Team (SAG) on Saturday afternoons, but some things are more important.

Even Kezia, yelling at me for going off again and taking her Heavenscent body-spray and Mum nagging me to remember that there's more to life than boys (such as ???!!!), fails to bring me down to earth.

'There's more to life than work, Mum!' I can't help saying. 'You said you'd like to meet the Right Man – remember? And now I've met the Right Boy!' It's hard to focus on my Resolution to Be Nice to Parents, Siblings, Tash and Teachers – my mind's in a whirl!

'You must introduce me to your boyfriend,' says Mum, alarmingly. I'm not sure I feel ready for this! 'But it's important to keep your feet on the ground.'

Impossible! My feet are at least sixteen centimetres off the ground as I float back to Sophie's house, where I find a worried-looking Kyle standing halfway down or up the stairs.

'There's something wrong with Sophie,' he says. 'She keeps SMILING at me – it's really freaking me out!'

I don't say anything – I just smile at him . . .

Rob and Luke are doing amazing things on their BMXes at the skate park, and a small crowd, which includes Kyle (who has brought his bike), has gathered to watch them.

Sophie and I are sitting a short distance apart from

ROB AND LUKE

everyone else, being cool and oozing pride that Rob and Luke are our boyfriends. I still can't believe it – it doesn't seem real . . .

'That was a tail whip,' says Sophie knowledgeably. 'It's a very hard trick – Luke's brilliant. Look at the way he's riding that grind rail.'

'Have you been logging on to bmxingforbeginners. com, or something?' I enquire. 'Or possibly reading *The Observer's Book of* BMX*ing*?'

'Yes.'

'I thought so.'

'I want to share his interest – no, his passion!' Sophie enthuses.

'I *know* you want to share his passion,' I say, giving her a playful push. She pushes me back, and we roll around on the grass, giggling – not quite as cool as we were.

Jasmine and Jocasta have appeared out of nowhere and are looking down their noses at us.

'The Weird Sisters at play,' Jasmine comments scornfully. 'How sweet!'

'Get lost, Jasmine,' Sophie yells at her as Jasmine glides away, laughing and whispering to Jocasta, and looking back over her shoulder.

'I *hate* that girl!' Sophie hisses, fiercely.

'Calm down, Sofe – she's no threat to you. I'm sure of that,' I say, reassuringly. 'Just ignore her. She's probably jealous of your cool hair, and the fact that Luke likes *you* better . . .'

But Sophie's early warning system is on full alert and her radar is locked onto Jasmine as Jasmine parades up and down (with her bum in full wiggle mode) where Luke can see her. I notice that he keeps looking at her – this must be worrying for Sophie – and then something distracts me.

'What *is* Kyle doing?' I ask.

He is riding his bike – which is not a BMX – at full speed towards a quarter pipe.

'I *think* he's showing off,' says Sophie. 'Look – there's a group of girls from his year. Oh, dear.'

Kyle has fallen off his bike – one of the girls has rushed forward to help him up.

'He's OK,' says Sophie. 'I wouldn't be surprised if he did that on purpose, to get attention. That girl who's tending his wounds and mopping his manly brow is called Charlotte Steel. She went to our house once to help him with his homework – at least, that's what they *said* they were doing . . . Wow! Kyle must have a girl-friend. Seriously weird!' But her gaze has already returned to Luke – and a hard stare for Jasmine . . .

1.30 p.m.

Rob and Luke have been BMXing for over an hour. The sun is shining, but I feel cold from sitting still, so I get up and wander up and down. Sophie says that she's thirsty. I tell her to go and get a drink from the leisure centre, which is beside the skate park. She replies that she's not going anywhere in case the Wicked Witch of the West – I assume that she means Jasmine – casts a spell on Luke while she's gone.

1.45 p.m.

Rob and Luke are still BMXing. I stifle a yawn.

'Are you bored?' asks Sophie, sharply.

'No.'

'Me neither. This is great, isn't it?'

'Yes.'

2.00 p.m.

The boys are still BMXing. Sophie says that she is hungry. I tell her to go and get a sandwich, and to get me one while she's at it. She refuses. Rob and Luke's admiring audience has dispersed, although a few other people have taken their place. Jasmine is looking sulky and not even attempting to disguise the fact that she is very, very BORED. Kyle – who bravely managed to sip a little of the water that Charlotte brought him from the leisure centre – has recovered sufficiently to eat the crisps and chocolate bars which she also brought him.

'Why don't *you* go and get the sandwiches?' Sophie snaps at me, suddenly.

'Why are you getting stressy?'

'It's because my blood sugar levels are low. That's what Mum says.'

I think it's Sophie's anxiety levels which are to blame. Jasmine won't go away, and Luke has smiled at her several times. He has also smiled at Sophie, and at Lydia, who was passing by, and at a group of girls who kept clapping every time he did a stunt . . .

2.10 p.m.

The boys have finished BMXing. I notice Sophie hastily stuff an extra-strong mint or two in her mouth and apply another layer of Cherrypie and Kiwi lip gloss.

What does she think is going to happen in the middle of the skate park? Or maybe she's trying to boost her blood sugar levels?

The boys flop down on the grass beside us.

'Are you OK, babe?' Rob asks me, reaching out and touching my hand.

'I'm . . .' My mind has gone blank – I cannot think of a single word which adequately sums up how I am feeling, apart from WHEEWHOOOWHAAA! But I had better not say that otherwise people will think I am strange.

Luke is lying on his front examining a small patch of grass. Sophie is sitting bolt upright beside him, looking uneasy, with a forced smile on her face. No wonder Kyle was scared. It isn't like her normal smile . . . I think Sophie needs to relax and stop worrying, so I wish Luke would stop smiling at other girls – uh oh, I have seen something which is SERIOUSLY not going to help.

Jasmine has joined us, with Jocasta in tow. She bears down on Luke with all-the-better-to-eat-you eyes, flashing him the ultimate seductive smile.

'Want to go for a walk?' she asks him.

Luke looks awkward, ducking his head as if avoiding a punch, but managing a shy smile. Oh, bother it! Poor Sophie.

'Come *on*!' Jasmine says, obviously getting impatient. 'We need to talk – I've got something to say. Unfinished business,' she adds, glaring at the rest of us (who she evidently considers far too boring to have things like unfinished business).

Without looking at Sophie, Luke gets to his feet and wanders off with Jasmine, who contents herself with a slight sneer at Sophie over her shoulder as she walks away. Jocasta follows Luke and Jasmine, trailing a few paces behind.

I feel sorry for Sophie – she doesn't deserve this.

'Don't let her get to you, Sofe,' I whisper, touching her hand. 'Jasmine's a cow – she's just winding you up. Luke'll be back in a minute.'

I want Rob to say something to reassure Sophie, but he doesn't. He just shakes his head and mutters a rude word under his breath. I wish I could think of something to say to break the silence.

'Anyone hungry?' Rob asks.

'I wouldn't say no to a sandwich,' I reply. 'I'll come with you to get them. Anything for you, Sofe?'

'Get me chocolate!' says Sophie, hoarsely. 'Lots of chocolate!'

We have eaten our sandwiches (bacon, lettuce and tomato for Rob; chicken tikka for me) and Sophie is halfway through her second chocolate bar when Luke returns, without Jasmine (or Jocasta).

'Did anyone get me a sandwich?' he asks, flopping down beside Sophie as if nothing has happened.

'Get your own,' says Rob, shortly. There seems to be an atmosphere between them. The weather has clouded over, and a thin wind is blowing. I begin to shiver.

'Don't worry, Rob,' says Luke. 'There's nothing going on between me and Jasmine. There can't be. It's over. I told her.'

Fine. That's OK, then. Thanks for telling us. But shouldn't he be saying this to Sophie, rather than to Rob? Luke may be shy, but at the moment he is also being insensitive. Sophie is sitting bolt upright again, looking hopeful – but still worried.

'It had better be over,' says Rob. Turning to me, he adds: 'She wanted Luke to give up his bike for her. How bad was that?'

'Pretty bad,' I agree.

'I would never do that!' Sophie exclaims – and immediately blushes full plum tomato. I want to give her a hug – it would be nice if *Luke* gave her a hug.

'*Nothing* and *no one* comes between us and our bikes,' Rob declares. I am beginning to feel that he could stop going on about it – I think we've got the message. I notice that Luke has gone back to studying his patch of grass. He doesn't seem as fired up as Rob.

'We call ourselves the Two Biketeers,' Rob continues.

I MUST NOT LOOK AT SOPHIE. I know that if I catch her eye, I will crack up and get the giggles – badly.

Although I suspect that she may not be in the mood for extreme mirth.

Fortunately, I am distracted for a moment by a text from Dad saying that he is looking forward to seeing me soon. I send one back to say that I am looking forward to seeing him, too.

Rob is still talking about BMXing.

'We're competing in the BMX championships in Loughborough next June, and we've got to get in some SERIOUS PRACTICE between now and then,' he says. 'Tomorrow's a big day for us because there's this amazing BMXer I know who's coming down from London to put us through our paces – we've got to be back here at eleven o'clock sharp tomorrow morning. OK, Luke?'

'Yes, whatever. But right now I need a break – I'm starving.' Sophie offers Luke her remaining chocolate bars, and he takes them with a shy smile. I can see Sophie visibly melt . . . 'Hey, weren't we going bowling?' he asks, trying to disguise the fact that he is blushing – so is Sophie. I suppose they do make a sweet couple, if only Luke could stop being distracted by other girls. 'Rob and I could take our bikes home, and meet you at the rink in about forty-five minutes, if you like.'

'Bowling. Cool!' enthuses a familiar voice. Kyle has walked up behind us – he is holding hands with a triumphant-looking Charlotte, who keeps looking back over her shoulder and mouthing things at her group of

KYLE WITH A GIRLFRIEND!

friends, who are giggling and giving her the thumbs-up.

'Want to go bowling, Chaz?' Kyle says to Charlotte, over-loudly and over-casually, trying to make his voice sound deeper than it really is. 'You guys don't mind if Chaz and me join you, do you?'

Sophie is mouthing 'No!' at Kyle, and fixing him with a look which says: I-WILL-KILL-YOU-LATER-AND-STUFF-YOUR-REMAINS-IN-A-BOX-AND-JUMP-UP-AND-DOWN-ON-IT!

'Feel free,' says Luke.

'Cool!' exclaims Kyle, forgetting to make his voice deeper. 'I still can't believe you're going out with my sister. I mean, *my* sister! MY SISTER! That's so weird.' He shakes his head and laughs, while Sophie dies quietly in the background.

* * *

'Have you finished murdering him yet?' I ask, when Sophie comes back into her room, where I am sprawled on the bed, reliving in my mind the enjoyable view I had of Rob's bum-to-die-for every time he bent over to bowl at the leisure centre this afternoon.

BEST MATES FOREVER!
WE CAN LAUGH ABOUT EVERYTHING TOGETHER!

'I told the horrid brat that he was never EVER to show off and embarrass me like that again,' Sophie replies. 'And then I murdered him.'

'I thought you'd made a Resolution to Be Nice to Parents, Siblings and Teachers.'

Sophie pulls a face. 'At least I kept *two* of my resolutions today,' she says. 'I gave my chocolate to Luke – that's "Giving to Others" and "Giving up Chocolate". Two for the price of one!'

I frown – there is something on my mind.

'Out with it,' says Sophie, cheerfully.

'Perhaps,' I say, slowly, 'perhaps Luke is the one you should murder – not poor little Kyle.'

'How can you say that?' Sophie exclaims. 'You heard Luke – there's *nothing* going on between him and Jasmine.'

'And you believe him?'

'YES! Stop trying to spoil my happiness. *You* said that Jasmine was just winding me up – remember?'

'I know . . . yes . . . I'm sure she was.' I don't want to upset Sophie – I can tell that she is desperate for me to reassure her – but the fact that she needs reassurance shows that she is feeling insecure. As her Best Mate Forever I feel I must tell her what I've noticed – that Luke keeps smiling at other girls – and it is hard to ignore the fact that he meekly followed after Jasmine, even if he *said* he's finished with her . . .

'It's just that . . . he doesn't seem completely *committed*,' I say, trying to be as tactful as possible. Judging by the look on Sophie's face, I am not succeeding.

'It's a bit early for commitment,' Sophie replies, shortly. 'We haven't even got to tongues yet.'

Before I can say anything else, Sophie has moved on – Gemini butterfly-style – to another subject, and her enthusiasm carries me along, as it so often does. She seems particularly bright and energetic, as if trying to block out more unsettling thoughts.

'Kyle lent me *this*,' she exclaims triumphantly, showing me Kyle's phone. She must have been scary for Kyle to agree to part with his phone – it is his pride and joy, with features including MP3 and take-photos-of-your-mates-pulling-faces facility.

'He's letting me borrow it just for tonight,' Sophie tells me. 'So I'll be able to use it to check my make-up and take photos TONIGHT!'

The word 'tonight' is heavy with significance because it is *tonight* that Sophie is going on a date with Luke on their own, and I am going on a date with Rob on *our* own – the boys asked us when we left the bowling alley. I think it was mainly Rob's idea; I think he is more serious about me than Luke is about Sophie. I am going to stay at Sophie's house again so that we can discuss our dates when we get back. It will be my last chance for a sleepover before I go to stay with Dad. I want to spend some time at home with Mum before I go, so I can make sure she's not too much of a Lonely Heart – I wonder if it's worth mentioning that the plumber doesn't wear a wedding ring?

I am looking forward to my sleepover with Sophie almost as much as I'm looking forward to my Date with Rob, though. I feel strangely nervous about being on my own with Rob, even though I've snogged him. What if I make a fool of myself by tripping over or saying something stupid? It is reassuring to think that I will be back with Sophie at the end of the evening – Best Mates Forever! We can laugh about everything together.

'TONIGHT,' says Sophie, relishing the word, 'TONIGHT I want to take photos of Luke, *and* I want to know what his star-sign is and whether he's a fire sign – or if he was born on the cusp, which might explain any indecisiveness – *and* I want to find out what's really going on inside his head, *and* I want to know, once and for all, that Jasmine is a thing of the past, *and* I want to know if there's a future for us, and if we can be More Than Just Good Friends.'

'Good luck,' I say. 'Tonight I want to snog.'

Sophie looks at me – and we both burst into fits of giggles.

'Oh, Tash!' Sophie gasps. 'I feel so much better now. I'm so glad you're my friend.'

'Me too.'

Chapter 6

Sophie

'I WANT A PHONE like Kyle's,' I exclaim. 'The only reason he got one before I did is because he's a spoilt brat.'

Tash and I have already had fun with the phone, taking close-ups of ourselves puckering up, pouting and posing like supermodels, ready for my date with destiny (or Luke).

'I had to promise to top it up if I use any of his credit,' I tell Tash. 'And he wanted me to add on ten pounds of interest, so I told him where I'd put his phone if he didn't shut up.'

'Ouch!'

'Yes – and the rest of my family is driving me mad, too. Every time I get a message on my phone, Mum goes: "Is it from *him*?" in this really silly voice.'

7.00 p.m.
Tash and I jostle to check our make-up in Kyle's phone

as Dad drives us to the mall, where we have agreed to meet the boys outside Froth's, before going our separate ways.

'Just drop us in the main car park, Dad – please,' I say. 'It's only a few minutes' extra to walk to the mall – we need the exercise. Young people need to take more exercise, don't they? Or they run the risk of developing life-threatening diseases in later life, such as . . .' I am trying to keep my Resolution to Be Nice to Parents, Siblings and Teachers, even if they *do* drive me mad.

'It's OK, Sophie,' says Dad. 'I *won't* embarrass you in front of your boyfriend. But I *will* wait with you until the boys arrive – and *no* arguments. And if you're not ready and waiting for me at the Market Cross at ten-thirty SHARP, as we agreed, I will get out of the car and cause you more embarrassment than you have ever experienced in your life before – is that understood? You have been warned.'

'TEN-THIRTY! That is so *early*,' I moan, as we wait outside Froth's for the boys to arrive. I have persuaded Dad to wait about ten paces away. Why is he so over-protective? I know that I am lucky to have a dad who cares – but you can take caring too far. I hope he isn't planning to come on the date WITH me. I pretend to be interested in the menu framed in a glass case beside the entrance.

'You don't think . . . you don't think they'd stand us up, do you?' Tash whispers, nervously.

'For God's sake, Tash! I've already got really bad butterflies, and you just made them swoop down to the pit of my stomach all at once.' I like it when Tash makes me laugh. I DON'T like it when she makes me feel insecure about Luke. I wish she'd STOP.

'Sorry. It's OK, I can see them,' Tash says.

'What – the butterflies?'

A HARD STARE IN THE DIRECTION OF THE BOYS...

'No, no. The *boys*! Sofe, I'm so nervous. Do I look mad? Be honest!'

'No madder than usual. Listen, we can text each other . . .' I signal frantically to Dad that he can leave. I try not to GLARE at him – I MUST keep my resolution! With a final hard stare in the direction of the boys, Dad turns and wanders slowly away.

7.10 p.m.

On my own with Luke at last. But I am so nervous that I keep wishing Tash were here, even if she *does* keep worrying me!

7.20 p.m.

Walking slowly down the mall with Luke, I check my reflection in shop windows as we pass. So far I have said, 'Hi!' and he has said, 'Hi!' I think I need to make progress if I am going to discover his innermost thoughts and feelings . . . Inspiration! I show him Kyle's phone. This breaks the ice. We take stupid photos of each other.

7.30 p.m.

On our way back up the other side of the mall we pass Rob and Tash going in the opposite direction. Tash grins at me. He has his arm round her shoulders, and – WOW! – she has her hand in the back pocket of his jeans. I am not jealous. I am *pleased* that Tash's date is going so well – she will probably have plenty to tell me later! I just hope that I have something to tell *her* – like how a heavenly choir sang and a thousand fireworks went off when I had that fabled and long-awaited First Kiss with Luke.

7.35 p.m.

'We could go back to my place, if you like,' Luke suggests, casually. 'It's only a few streets away.' My heart skips a beat – this is surely something to tell Tash. But will his parents be there? 'Mum and Dad are out,' says Luke, apparently reading my mind – a sure sign that we are soul mates. 'So we'll have the place to ourselves, more or less.' But I hope he can't read my mind ALL the time. Some of my thoughts should be censored . . .

7.55 p.m.

A light drizzle is falling when we reach Luke's house, which is in the middle of a terraced row of three-storey buildings. A thin but strong autumn breeze whips the drizzle into my face, and I wish I'd worn a thicker jacket over my white V-neck top and fucshia-pink trousers. I got bored with black – it wasn't really me – but I am worried that the pink trousers clash with my hair. At least it shows that I am a colourful character.

There seems to be an absence of parents at Luke's house – just as he said – so no one sees us as we climb the stairs to his room. I-AM-GOING-INTO-HIS-ROOM!!! My heart is beating so loudly that I am sure he must be able to hear it, and there are things with wings in my stomach. I think we are definitely taking our relationship up a level – or two, as his bedroom is on the third floor.

Most of the available space in Luke's room is taken up by two sets of metal-framed bunk beds, leaving just enough room for a chest of drawers, on top of which is a television and PlayStation. There is an overwhelming smell of socks, mingled with bodyspray – it is like Kyle x four.

'Do you share?' I ask.

'Three brothers. All older. All out.'

'Why are you all in one room?'

'I've got three sisters too. All older. All out. Then Mum and Dad have a room, and Uncle Stu's in the basement.'

'Big family!'

'Yup. What would you like to play on? This one's good.' Luke shows me a PlayStation game called *Extreme BMXing*. I say, 'Cool,' because I want to show that I don't mind at all that he is totally obsessed by BMXing, and then I ask where the bathroom is. While I am in the bathroom I send a text to Tash which says, 'Gone back to Luke's place.' This sounds good, and should make her realise that she is not the only one having fun.

8.30 p.m.

Luke has been playing on *Extreme BMXing* for half an hour without saying a word, apart from asking me if I'd like a drink from a half-empty two-litre bottle of Coke, which I politely decline, wondering how many people

LUKE HAS BEEN PLAYING ON 'EXTREME BMXing'
FOR HALF AN HOUR ...

have drunk from it. He also offers me an extra-strong mint. Does this mean what I think it does?

8.45 p.m.

Apparently not. Doesn't he fancy me any longer? Or . . . maybe Tash is right and he's afraid of commitment – or maybe his feelings for me are so strong that he is SCARED. And he *is* shy, after all . . . But time is ticking by, and I can't help feeling impatient. Here we are in his room (on our own) and the stage is set for that First Kiss, but Luke seems to have missed his cue. I clear my throat nervously . . .

'Have you and Rob been friends for long?' I ask, trying to distract him from the PlayStation. (He could play on *that* any time.)

'Yes – forever. We've known each other since nursery school – there are photos of us zooming around on tricycles together.'

'And now it's BMXes.'

'Yes.'

I am puzzled by a note of resignation in Luke's voice.

'Rob said that you don't let anyone or anything come between you and your bikes.'

'That's Rob's approach.'

'Not yours?'

'It used to be. But now I think there's more to life.'

'Such as?' I am getting closer to the real Luke.

'Such as going out with girls . . . er . . . er . . . I mean . . . with you,' Luke manages to tear his gaze away from *Extreme* BMX*ing* for the first time in nearly an hour, and gives me a nervous smile – he is blushing. My heart performs an extreme stunt, and I think I am blushing, too. But I am worried – how many girls does he want to go out with?

'So wh . . . why did you say you wanted to be Just Good Friends?' I ask, tentatively. Then: 'Do you still fancy Jasmine?' I blurt out.

'N–no!' He is ducking his head, as if avoiding punches.

'You don't seem very sure . . .' Oh dear! Am I pressurising him? I'll drive him away. But I'm worried about those 'girls' he mentioned. Especially Jasmine . . .

'I *am* sure,' Luke exclaims, sounding almost angry.

Have I upset him? 'Look – I'll prove it to you. We'll spend the day together tomorrow,' he says.

'But Rob said you've got to be at the skate park . . .'

'Rob can't control my life – he just tries to! That's why I said I wanted to be Just Good Friends – because he was there, and I didn't want him knowing everything about my life.'

'Look – I don't want to cause problems between you two . . .'

'There are no problems – only solutions,' Luke says emphatically, putting down his PlayStation controller.

'MMRFF!' This is the sound I make because I have just opened my mouth to say something when I find

NOT QUITE THE ROMANTIC KISS
I'D BEEN HOPING FOR!

Luke's tongue almost touching my tonsils. I can taste Coke and extra-strong mint – and I can't breathe . . . My eyes are wide open.

After conducting a short but thorough internal examination of my mouth with his tongue, Luke stops kissing me, gives me a smile and a friendly pat on the shoulder, and goes back to playing on the PlayStation. He is blushing . . .

'I . . . er . . . I need the bathroom,' I manage to say, walking unsteadily from the room. It was not how I had imagined my First Kiss – where was the heavenly choir? What happened to the fireworks? My cheeks are burning! But – wait a minute! – Luke KISSED me! He must *really* like me. And it wasn't *that* bad, I suppose – at least my teeth didn't get in the way! Perhaps we just need to practise! I *must* text Tash . . . Luke and I are officially MTJGF!!!

Chapter 7

Natasha

7.10 p.m.

AFTER WE HAVE SPLIT UP from Sophie and Luke, Rob takes me to look in the window of a cycle shop. I am alone on a date with my Fate Mate at last.

'Look at the wheels on that!' he enthuses, pointing to a black BMX and drooling slightly. 'Serious stunt pegs.'

I am drooling slightly too, but not because of the bike. I lurve being close to Rob, and my happiness is complete when he puts his arm around me. I am not sure what to do with my own arms – they suddenly seem too long – and then I remember seeing girls with their hands in boys' back pockets. I move my arm behind Rob – what if he doesn't have a back pocket? He might think I'm groping his bum. To my relief, it doesn't take too much feeling my way around before I find his back pocket, and slip my hand into it . . . OHMIGOD, I HAVE MY HAND ON ROB'S BUM. I can't *wait* to tell Sophie about *this*!!!

7.30 p.m.

We pass Sophie and Luke going the other way. Her eyes come out on stalks so I think she must have noticed my hand in his back pocket.

7.45 p.m.

We meet Kezia and Geoffrey. *And* Mum. Aaaaargh!!! I quickly extract my hand from Rob's back pocket.

'Tash, fancy seeing *you!*' Kezia exclaims, not looking at me. Her eyes are fixed on Rob. 'Are you going to introduce me?'

Do I *need* to?

'We've heard all about you,' says Mum, giving Rob a searching look. It is always worrying when people say this – what have they heard?

Rob grins nervously.

'Come and have tea one day,' says Mum. Tea? What sort of tea? Does she mean one of her famous, burnt microwave pizzas? Or the tea you drink? Mum never drinks tea. 'I'm afraid I've got to dash,' she continues. 'I've been late-night shopping with Kezia, and now I've got to get to the supermarket before it closes – or we won't have any tea. Ha ha!'

OK, so where did the strange obsession with tea come from? And the manic laugh? Mum gives me a kiss, looks into my eyes and tells me to 'Take care' and not be late. She reminds me to call her as soon as I get back – then she dashes away . . . Thank goodness! That's one mad family member out of the way – which leaves my strange sister . . .

7.50 p.m.
I wish Kezia would stop staring at Rob. He is beginning to shift uneasily from one foot to the other, clearing his throat and looking around – probably for an escape route.

Geoffrey suggests that we all go for a drink. This seems like a good idea until Kezia hisses: 'Don't be silly, Geoffrey – they're under-age.'

I WISH KEZIA WOULD STOP STARING AT ROB...

Suddenly I feel about six years old. Thanks, Kez!

'Not to worry,' says Geoffrey, good-humouredly. 'I know where we can go – they've got live jazz at Froth's tonight.' Froth's has become quite an 'in place' recently, staying open late on Fridays and Saturdays and attracting students from Bodmington College like Kezia and Geoffrey.

On our way to Froth's, Kezia takes me to one side and tells me that Dad phoned earlier to confirm the arrangement we made for me to stay with him from Monday until Wednesday next week. Mum will drive me halfway, and Dad will meet us and take me the rest of the way. Kezia tells me that Dad was 'worried' when he heard that I had gone on a date, and said that he would ring me on my mobile. He hasn't yet . . . It's half reassuring and half annoying that he is worried about me. I send him a message to say that I'm OK. Dad and I often exchange messages on our mobiles – it helps me to feel close to him.

Taking me by the arm and leaning close to me, Kezia says, in an audible whisper: 'Rob's very good-looking, Tash. What a *bum*! Sexeee, or what? But be careful – make sure you take PRECAUTIONS!' She hisses this last word so loudly that I am sure I hear it echoing all the way down the mall, and back – and *everyone*, including Rob, looks at me. I want to die. My sister obviously thinks that I am a sex maniac – and now so does everyone else. I sympathise with Sophie's desire to murder Kyle – I feel the same about Kezia. But murdering our siblings wouldn't fit with Sophie's Resolution to Be Nice to Parents, Siblings and Teachers.

8.00 p.m.
The live jazz band at Froth's is called Full Blast – and it

certainly is! I can't hear myself speak over the screeching of the saxophone. Geoffrey is yelling at me – something about SEX!!! Oh no! Don't tell me *he's* going to have a go at me about taking precautions – how mega EMBARRASSING.

'Great *sax*,' Geoffrey repeats, realising that I haven't heard him properly. Phew! What a relief . . .

'Latte?' Geoffrey shouts, looking at me and Rob.

'Not for me!' I yell back, but Geoffrey hasn't heard me. He has gone to fetch me a latte.

GREAT SAX !

9.00 p.m.
Rob and I have said goodbye to Kezia and Geoffrey because we want to go for a walk on our own, and I couldn't stand any more live Jazz, or drink any more of my latte. But it was fun playing footsie with Rob under the table.

Kezia yells at me not to be back at Sophie's house

too late or she'll tell Mum and I'll be grounded. She seems determined to make me look and feel about six years old in front of Rob – I expect she's jealous because my boyfriend is better-looking than hers. And she won't *know* how late I get back, anyway.

There is a ringing in my ears and I feel deafened by all that 'great sax'! Checking my phone, I see that I have a message – is it from Dad? But it turns out to be from Sophie, to say that she has gone back to Luke's place. Is she trying to impress me? Well, I *am* impressed . . . sort of. I wonder if Rob will invite me back to *his* place? I wonder why Dad hasn't replied to my message – perhaps he's changing a nappy.

'Hello?' Rob is looking at me enquiringly. We are in a dark, almost-deserted corner of the mall.

'Oh, sorry. I was miles away!'

'Then you'd better come a bit closer.' Rob pulls me towards him. My knees are jelly, my stomach is doing slow cartwheels, my mind is whirling. My phone rings.

Rob lets go, while I answer my phone.

'Oh, hi, Dad!' Although he sends messages, Dad doesn't often ring me on my mobile – what a moment to choose. I'm glad he doesn't know that I was within seconds of going into total snog mode.

'I'm fine. How are you? And Alfie? I'm with Rob . . . yes . . . yes . . . no . . . no . . . NO! . . . I'm OK, Dad – honestly. No – I won't be back late . . . OK . . . OK – I'll ring you as soon as I get back. Promise! Love you! Bye!'

'That was my dad,' I explain to Rob, unnecessarily.

'Where were we?' says Rob, drawing me to him.

His lips are closing in on my lips . . . I close my eyes . . . my phone rings . . .

Rob lets go, rolls his eyes, and goes to look in the window of a nearby shop while I answer my phone. It is Sophie in hyper-excited motor-mouth mode: 'I'm in Luke's bathroom. I'm holding a rubber ducky. I don't know what I'm doing. I don't know what I'm saying. He *kissed* me, Tash! He *kissed* me! Not on the cheek. PROPER KISSING. And my teeth didn't get in the way. It was AMAZING! Sort of strange but . . . AMAZING! But I forgot to close my eyes – and I couldn't breathe – and I think I'm going to have to try it again to get it right, and . . .'

'Sophie! *Sophie*! I'm pleased for you, honey, but I've got to go.' Sophie has given me an ear sweat.

'You *could* switch it off,' Rob suggests.

'Yes,' I agree. 'I suppose I could.'

'Now – where were we . . .?'

Chapter 8
Sophie

I WAS TWENTY MINUTES late getting to the Market Cross to meet Dad, and Tash was half an hour late. What was she doing? I intend to find out. And I can't wait to tell her that Luke and I are *serious* – so she was wrong to have doubts about him.

Dad went mad – he was furious. But nothing can upset me – I am floating! I point out that it wasn't *my* fault that Dad left his phone at home, so I couldn't let him know that I'd be late because I was too busy having my face snogged off. Luke kissed me once more when I got back from the bathroom, and it was better because I remembered to close my eyes and breathe – but then we had to stop because his parents got back . . .

Dad has grounded me indefinitely and banned me from having boyfriends until I am twenty-one. Talk about unfair! I argued and whinged (I don't get away with this sort of behaviour with Mum, but it sometimes works with Dad because he can't stand it, and ends up agreeing to anything just to stop me carrying on . . . I KNOW I am breaking my Resolution to Be Nice to Parents, Siblings and Teachers – but I *must* see Luke). Eventually Dad said that it was OK for Luke to come to our house tomorrow. This means that he runs the risk of encountering members of my weird family. I don't know how he will cope with this – but I don't think I can survive a day without seeing him.

I remind Dad that Tash and I are meant to be walking Crumpet the dog tomorrow afternoon. We do this every Sunday before going back to have tea and biscuits with Crumpet's owner, Mrs Ames, and her elderly mother who Tash and I refer to as Granny – she is a kind, sweet old lady, and we are very fond of her.

'Whatever . . .' says Dad, wearily. I have CONTROL! Tash and I spend the rest of the journey whispering about our Dates, telling each other to 'Ssh' and giggling at the photos I took on Kyle's phone of Luke and me mucking around. I remind Dad to keep his eyes on the road.

'So?' I ask Tash, eagerly back upstairs in my room, as soon as she has finished phoning her dad to tell him she's OK. It turns out that he was about to phone her mum because he was getting seriously worried. Tash had already phoned her mum. She seemed worried that Kezia was going to get her grounded.

'So what?' Tash asks.

'So what *happened*? Durrr! Come on, girl! It's SAYS time, now that Dad isn't around.'

'I told you,' Tash replies. 'We snogged – that's all.'

'That's ALL?! Do you . . . er . . . do you do tongues?' I ask, hesitantly.

Tash screams with laughter and I tell her to 'Sssh.'

'Oh, yes,' she replies. 'Tongues, teeth, tonsils, twiddly bits – the lot.'

I want to ask about the 'twiddly bits' but another question occurs to me. 'Why did you turn your phone off?' I ask.

'Because *you* wouldn't stop phoning me. You were giving me *serious* ear sweats.'

'I only phoned you *once*!'

'Yes, but I *knew* you'd phone again! Rob said to switch it off. And he said I was worth waiting for.'

'Luke said I was really good at kissing.'

'Rob said I was a super-sexy red-hot babe with the most snoggable mouth in the universe.'

I shriek with laughter. 'Luke said . . . Luke said I had a nice smile.'

'He said that before,' says Tash, giggling. We can't *stop* giggling.

'He said it again. Then his mum and dad came back

and they were really nice, and his mum made us cocoa, and she kept calling me by the wrong name – probably because they've got so many children – Luke's the youngest of seven. But they seemed to like me, and then Luke walked me back to the Market Cross.'

'Rob said I had beautiful eyes . . .' I don't think Tash has been listening to a word I said. She is seriously obsessed! All she can say is, 'Rob says . . .' I feel vaguely irritated – I want her to be interested in how *my* date went; I asked about *hers*. Am I imagining things or are we drifting apart into two separate worlds? I seriously don't want that to happen.

'I've just texted Luke,' I say, banishing dark thoughts from my mind. 'I want to get him over here tomorrow – although I must be mad. I hope Dad doesn't want to have "a little chat" with him.'

'But isn't he meant to be meeting Rob at the skate park?' says Tash. 'Rob said it was really crucial that Luke showed up because this BMX person from London can only come tomorrow.'

'Luke said that Rob can't control his life. He said that he wanted to spend the day with me tomorrow to prove that he's serious about me,' I reply.

'Rob said that he wanted me to go to the skate park tomorrow to watch him,' says Tash. 'But I'm not going if it means I'm going to have to explain about Luke not showing up.'

'I'm sure they can sort it out between them,' I exclaim. 'Perhaps Luke can go along to the skate park for part of the day, or something.' My phone beeps. 'Oh, wow! He says he *will* come here tomorrow! We're going to meet at the Joyful Shopper Minimart – he knows where that is – at eleven o'clock, and walk the rest of the way. Oh, Tash. Isn't it wonderful? Being IN LURVE!!!'

'Yes, but I still think it's going to cause problems when Luke doesn't show up. You're not making it very easy for Rob and me!' Tash says, accusingly.

'What do you mean? It was Luke's idea to see me tomorrow – you make me sound like some sort of traitor. Can't you be pleased for me? I'm confused.'

CAN'T YOU BE PLEASED FOR ME?

'You're always confused, Sophie,' says Tash, with a shrug. Then she says that it doesn't matter, and she's just worried about her mum being a Lonely Heart, especially as she's about to leave her to go to stay with her dad.

'So, I've got other stuff on my mind,' says Tash, making

it sound as though I *haven't*. Of all the – !!! Only my Resolution to Be Nice stops me from having a go at her.

Making an effort, I ask if there is anything I can do to help (remembering my Resolution to Give to Others).

'Have your parents got any unmarried male friends?' Tash asks.

'Er . . . there's one called Tim,' I reply. 'But he's mainly interested in stamps. And he keeps a boa constrictor in the bath.'

'No wonder he's unmarried. I don't think Mum could cope with that. Neither could I. Maybe Mum will meet someone on a business trip one day.'

Tash says she's tired, and wants to go to sleep. Why does she have to be in a mood? I want to do hand-springs round the room whenever I think about Luke, and I can't *wait* to get in some more kissing practice. I wonder what the twiddly bits are? But Tash is too tired and grumpy to tell me. I feel annoyed with her for making me feel guilty about seeing Luke tomorrow . . .

'Tomorrow everything will be fine,' I say. 'You'll see!'

Chapter 9

Natasha

I HAVE A BAD feeling about today.

'Life is GOOD!' Sophie exclaims, dancing round the room, hugging her phone. Kyle demanded *his* phone back the moment we got in through the door last night, and Sophie's mum, who was cross and worried, made her give it to him. Sophie begged him to save the photos of Luke for her – I expect he will, as Luke seems

to be his hero. 'Just an hour to go till I meet Luke at the Joyful Shopper Minimart,' Sophie trills.

'Just an hour to go before Rob seriously loses it,' I comment. 'Do you realise I can't go to the skate park because of you?'

'Why are you *still* in such a mood?' Sophie asks. 'I told you – *they'll sort it out*! As Luke says, "There are no problems – only solutions". I MUST remember to ask him what his star sign is – I'm sure he *must* be Leo.'

Can't she say anything apart from 'Luke says . . .' She is totally obsessed, and seems to have lost the ability to think for herself. She also seems to have lost the ability to spare a thought for *me*. I am beginning to resent her relationship with Luke – I want the old Sophie back! She wasn't *that* helpful about the Mum/Lonely Heart Situation – the old Sophie would have got out her star charts and found Mum's complementary star sign and worked out the ideal time/place, etc. to meet him.

'Now that we're going steady, I suppose it *is* about time I brought him home to meet the family,' Sophie rambles on. 'After all, I've met *his* parents.'

'Going steady? Hang on, girl!' I exclaim. 'You've been on two dates, Sofe. Or three, if you include bowling with Kyle, or watching them on their BMXes.'

'That's four, I think. How many dates do *you* think you need to go on before you can say you're going steady?'

'Four, I suppose. Or six. Maybe twelve. I don't *know*!' She is getting on my nerves – too much Luke.

Sophie has gone to meet Luke at the Joyful Shopper Minimart. Has she lost her psychic powers? I seem to be the only one with a bad feeling about today. I think that Sophie's all-seeing third eye has been temporarily – I hope – blinded by lurve . . . or by lust . . . I still have my doubts about Luke . . . and I still feel resentful . . .

I decide to go home to Mum because I miss her. Unfortunately she is in Full Nag Mode, telling me off for worrying her last night. Sophie and I got the same telling-off from Sophie's mum – the path of true lurve certainly doesn't run straight. Mum says that she wants to see me staying in a lot more, doing my homework. I wish I could think of *something* or someone that would help Mum to lighten up. Wouldn't it be nice if she said or did something to cheer *me* up? There doesn't seem to be much chance of *that*.

Mum tells me that she has to go to a conference on Tuesday in Scotland, and that it will involve her staying at a hotel for one night – but it won't affect me as I will be staying with Dad on that night, and Kezia will have Geoffrey for company. Mum tells me that she will be back late on Wednesday – Kezia, who is on half-term from Bodmington College, will collect me from Dad's house on Wednesday morning and bring me back.

I didn't expect Mum to go on a business trip so soon – perhaps she'll meet someone and become romantically involved with him. Am I ready for this? I don't know but I'm prepared to make an effort for Mum's sake. It will be great to see Dad (this is a cheering thought), but *how* will I survive three days away from Rob? THREE DAYS! Parting is 'such sweet sorrow'. I suppose we can text – and they *do* say that 'absence makes the heart grow fonder'! I will have to break the news to him gently . . . But what if he meets someone else while I'm gone? Aaargh!

'I'll have a colleague with me when I get back,' I hear Mum say, as I tune back into the Here and Now. 'He's going to have dinner with us and stay the night – he said he'd sleep on the sofa . . . He has to catch a plane early the next morning.'

So this is it. Mum hasn't even gone yet, and already she's bringing someone back! This is all happening a lot faster than I'd anticipated!

'Is he nice, Mum?' I ask.

'Er, yes,' Mum replies, sounding surprised. 'He's very . . . nice.'

VERY nice!!! Ohmigod! I must fight my fear of the unknown and help to welcome Mum's chance of happiness into our home. I have an idea – but I will need Sophie's help . . .

* * *

But there are even more immediate problems looming and weighing on my mind as I walk back to Sophie's house, and I am not as optimistic as Sophie (typical Gemini) about finding solutions . . .

My phone rings at 11.15 a.m. (as I thought it would).

'Hi, Rob.'

'Where the *hell* is Luke?' Rob demands, his angry voice drilling a hole in my eardrum. It would be nice if he said 'Hi.' I want to ask him if he enjoyed the date – but now doesn't seem like the right moment. 'He's supposed to *be* here!' Rob continues. 'His phone's switched off so I can't contact him! Sorry to shout at you – but do you know where he is? I phoned his mum and dad, and they seemed to think he'd gone to see a girl, only they weren't sure which one . . . I don't know which one, either – he got me to tell three different girls last week that he fancied them. They all love him because he's got looks and he's this shy guy – and he can't resist flirting – through ME! – and he doesn't know how to say no, so then he runs away, like now. AND HE'S DROPPED ME IN IT AND I'M NOT PUTTING UP WITH IT ANY MORE!'

I am speechless. I wasn't expecting such an explosion of feelings – and I'm devastated because I know Sophie will be heartbroken if all this is true, and I suspect that it is . . .

'I'll . . . I'll let you know if I see him, Rob. Rob?'

Rob has ended the call – he didn't even say 'goodbye'. I have just walked into Sophie's room. She and Luke are sitting on her bed, and they spring apart, obviously thinking that I am Sophie's mum or dad.

'Rob's furious with you,' I say to Luke. 'He just called me.' I am finding it hard to even look at Luke, let alone be polite to him.

Luke looks awkward, ducking his head in that way he does, as if dodging punches.

'Why don't you call him?' I say, sharply. 'I'm not going to be dropped in the middle of things like this – it's nothing to do with me. It's between you and Rob.'

'Er . . . Tash is right – it might help to . . . to clear the air,' Sophie says, tentatively. She looks at me nervously – I am obviously making her feel uneasy – but none of this is really *her* fault. I think she wants to make things right between us, which is a good sign – the old Sophie is still there. Relieved, I give her a smile and mouth: 'BMF!' She smiles back.

Luke shrugs his shoulders. 'OK,' he says. 'I suppose I'd better get this over with.' He goes out of the room and down the stairs with his phone. 'Hello? Rob?' we hear him say before he goes outside.

Sophie and I look at each other, and she starts giggling. 'Honestly,' she says. 'BOYS!'

'A couple of idiots, aren't they?' I say, nervously. 'I mean, what are they *like*?' I am not going to say anything right now about Rob's outburst. I don't want to hurt Sophie's feelings – and I suppose it's possible that Rob *might* have been saying those things because he was angry.

We sit side by side on the edge of the bed in silence, listening . . . I hear Luke's raised voice – I can't make out what he is saying, but he sounds angry.

'Oh, dear,' says Sophie.

Luke storms back into the room with a face like thunder and flings his phone down onto the bed. Sophie flinches and looks shocked – she is not used to seeing him like this.

'That's IT,' Luke bellows. 'I told Rob EXACTLY where he could PUT HIS STUNT PEGS!'

Silence. The seconds tick by . . .

Kyle pokes his head around the door.

'Oh, *no*,' I hear Sophie mutter under her breath. 'W*hy* didn't someone strangle him at birth?'

'I *thought* I heard your voice,' Kyle exclaims, gazing at Luke admiringly. 'Nothing wrong, is there? Wow! It's so cool that you're here – in my sister's room. Do you think you might have a chance to show me some stunts later?'

Sophie is shaking her head frantically at Kyle and mouthing 'NO!'

We hear footsteps on the stairs, and Sophie's mum's

voice approaching: 'Are you there. Sophie? I bought you a value pack of tampons at the Minimart! Dad and I popped down there to get newspapers and ice cream for lunch, and they were on special offer. I thought they'd be useful – here they are . . . oh! I didn't know you had company. Is this your . . . I mean . . . you must be Luke. Nice to meet you, Luke!'

I notice that Sophie and Luke have both blushed beetroot.

Sophie's mum invites Luke and me to stay for lunch, but I say that Mum is expecting me back, and I thank Sophie's mum for having me to stay. I want to talk to Rob and find out what's going on – were the things he said about Luke true? Or is Luke more serious about Sophie than about all those other girls – my one remaining hope. I don't want Sophie to be hurt, and I'd like us to be able to go on more Double Dates together

– so I also want to know if Rob and Luke are going to sort things out between them.

I tell Sophie in a whisper that I'm going to look for Rob, and that I'll meet her at Mrs Ames's house at three o'clock this afternoon so that we can walk Crumpet. It is somehow reassuring to have something 'normal' to look forward to.

Rob is at the skate park with a man wearing a grey hoodie and three-quarter-length grey shorts and a grey cap, grey socks and grey trainers. I assume that this must be the BMXer from London. He is shouting things out while Rob performs a series of amazing stunts.

Eventually Rob stops for a drink from his sports bottle, while the BMXer from London goes over to the leisure centre.

'Hi, Rob,' I say, going over to him.

'Oh, hi,' he says, sounding out of breath.

'You're . . . er . . . getting on OK without Luke,' I say, hopefully.

'No – total waste of time,' Rob replies, shortly.

'Oh . . .'

'We're *supposed* to be a team. We're supposed to *train* as a team. We're the Two Biketeers – the One Biketeer doesn't sound right, does it? It sounds stupid!'

'Er . . .'

'Luke's really let me down this time – and he *keeps*

doing it. He does it to girls, too – you know he's two-timing Sophie?'

'Oh, no!' This is worse than I suspected.

'I thought it was pretty obvious – he's still seeing Jasmine. And there are a couple of others, like I said . . . But he couldn't resist Sophie because she flirted with him and he *loves* flirty girls . . . For God's sake! He *knows* how important this is to me. I *thought* he was meant to be my friend.'

Rob looks so hurt. I feel really sorry for him – and I am so *angry* with Luke that I can't speak. The dishonest, cheating, heart-mangling, cowardly LOVE RAT! Poor Sophie! And how *could* he let down his Best Mate like this? POOR ROB! I shall *have* to tell Sophie . . . I just need to find the right moment.

I stay to watch Rob on his bike for a while – then I tell him that I have to go and do some coursework, but I might see him later. He says that he would like that very much.

Chapter 10

Sophie

LUKE IS QUIET AND SUBDUED while we are having lunch, and he doesn't eat much. I feel angry with Rob for upsetting him – and spoiling my day.

'Are you feeling OK, Luke?' Mum asks, in a concerned voice.

'Oh, yes. I'm fine, thank you – it was a lovely lunch.'

Mum and Dad's voices float out from the kitchen as Luke and I leave the house. Kyle has already gone to meet Charlotte at the skate park – I think he is planning to have another 'accident' . . .

'Luke seems like a nice, quiet, polite, well brought-up young man,' says Dad.

'Yes, I thought he seemed nice,' says Mum. 'But he didn't eat much – I think he was shy. A sensitive soul, like Sophie, inclined to daydream but always thinking of others.'

Don't they realise that Luke has EARS that he can HEAR WITH?

Turning round, I realise that Luke is already walking down the path and out onto the pavement, talking on his mobile.

'Is that Rob?' I ask, catching him up.

Luke hurriedly puts his phone away. 'N . . . no . . . That was Mum . . . Nothing important.' He looks at me. 'I really . . . er . . . like you,' he says, shyly. My heart flips like a fish. 'I don't mean to be such a . . . a . . .'

'Shy guy?' I suggest.

Luke opens his mouth to say something – then seems to change his mind.

'I'm shy, too,' I say cheerfully, to put him at his ease. I really feel that I am keeping all my resolutions at the moment. I am kind, supportive, caring – I even ate my ice cream *without* chocolate sauce.

I ask Luke if he'd like to walk Crumpet with me and Tash – he says that he would, as long as Rob isn't with Tash . . .

We get talking about the situation with Rob. Luke explains that he feels bullied by Rob, and he thought that the time had come to stand up to him. I tell him that he was right to do this as I can't *stand* bullying – there is nothing worse.

Tash is waiting for us outside Mrs Ames's house – there

is no sign of Rob. This is just as well because I think I might have had a go at him for bullying poor Luke. I am almost disappointed not to have the opportunity to do this, although I don't want to upset Tash.

Tash is being very abrupt towards Luke – I don't think this is very nice of her, and I don't know what her problem is, although she can be moody and difficult – *so* Sagittarius. But – again keeping my resolutions – I make an effort to be understanding. Perhaps she is still worried about her mum. And I have smiled at her – I still want us to be BMF more than anything.

Fortunately, the arrival of Crumpet on the scene causes everyone to forget their troubles for a while, as his boundless energy and enthusiasm for life (including chasing squirrels, the neighbour's cat, and peeing on every bush, tree or lamppost he passes) is infectious.

CRUMPET AND NEXT DOOR'S CAT

We are all exhausted when we get back to Mrs Ames's house, and Luke and I sink gratefully into Granny's comfortable sofa, while Tash helps her to bring in the tea and biscuits.

'So this is your young man!' says Granny, beaming at Luke. Does she think that Tash and I share him? I know that we share most things, but there is a limit . . . 'You

GRANNY MEETS LUKE

remind me a little of a young man called Gareth – I think you girls had quite a crush on young Gareth, didn't you?' Tash blushes furiously, and I am grinning like an idiot. 'And you also remind me of someone else,' Granny continues. 'Now – who was it? I know! Fred Winterbottom. He was a young man I used to know when I was a girl. Only his hair was shorter than yours. Fred and I went courting, but Father wasn't happy about it. He said that Fred was a ladies' man – and Father was right. Fred ran off with Elsie Blenkinsop who did the laundry. I heard that he got Elsie into trouble, and then he left her . . . You can do without men like Fred Winterbottom.'

I hear Tash mutter, 'Go, Granny!' under her breath – what *is* her problem?

'HAVE A BISCUIT!'

'But I'm sure that *you're* not like Fred Winterbottom,' says Granny, leaning forward and patting Luke's knee. 'You're a nice young man! Have a biscuit.'

* * *

Luke has to rush outside to take a call on his mobile (I expect he can't get a good signal inside the house). When he returns, he tells us that it was his mum, and he has to go home for his tea. Tash gives him a strange look . . . WHY? I *trust* Luke – I really do! Tash seems to want to drag me down – perhaps she's jealous because Rob isn't as SERIOUS about *her* as Luke is about ME. Rob wasn't willing to sacrifice a day's BMXing for *her*! I don't *want* to feel like this, but it's hard to be happy for Tash when she refuses to be happy for *me*.

After we have helped Granny clear away the tea things, we say goodbye and I go back to Tash's house to help her pack for going to stay with her dad tomorrow.

'Why did you give poor Luke that filthy look?' I can't help asking her. 'You were getting at him all afternoon – why?'

'You don't want to know,' Tash replies, shortly. It is mega annoying when people say this when you've just asked them a question – all it means is that they don't want to answer.

'I *do* want to know.' I feel my Resolution to Be Nice slipping . . .

'OK, Luke really upset Rob – he let him down badly,' Tash says. 'Rob said he's done it before. He's supposed to be Rob's friend.'

'Luke said Rob's a bully,' I retort.

'*Rob's* not a bully! He's kind and loyal, unlike Luke . . .'

'WHAT DO YOU MEAN?' I exclaim. My Resolution to Be Nice to Parents, Siblings, Honorary Siblings Such As Tash, and Teachers has just fallen to the ground and shattered into a million pieces.

'Luke cheats on girls. He's going behind your back with Jasmine – and with others . . . Rob said so. I'm sorry, Sofe.'

'You're not sorry,' I say, bitterly. 'Do you seriously believe EVERYTHING Rob says? He probably just said it out of spite because he was peed off with Luke. All you can ever say these days is, "*Rob* says . . ." Can't you think for yourself? It's "Yes, Rob, no, Rob, three bags full, Rob".'

'What about *you*? You're seriously OBSESSED, and you lap up every little lie he feeds you! Jasmine's probably

BMNF (BEST MATES NOT FOREVER?)

laughing her head off at you – I expect Luke's with her RIGHT NOW!!!'

'You're HORRIBLE! I'm *glad* you're going away!' I yell at Tash.

Fighting back the tears, I storm out of the house and all the way back home. I send a text to Luke to ask him if he is OK . . . then I try to ring him . . . his phone is switched off . . . there could be any number of reasons for this, all of them perfectly innocent . . . BOTHER Tash for making me feel suspicious and insecure. She had no RIGHT to do that! I thought she was my friend . . . my Best Mate Forever . . . or Not Forever . . . my BMNF!

I feel so angry. And lonely.

Chapter 11

Natasha

SO I WAS RIGHT TO have a bad feeling about yesterday.

Mum is concerned as she drives me to meet Dad because I am so quiet. Parents tell you off for making too much noise – and then they get concerned when you're quiet . . .

'Are you OK, darling?'

'I'm fine, Mum. Things on my mind, that's all.'

I wonder if I should try to talk to her about the things on my mind, which are as follows:

Thing On My Mind Number 1: Sophie had no RIGHT to call Rob a bully. And she made me sound like a total airhead with no mind of my own – I THOUGHT she was my FRIEND. I am so ANGRY! She and Luke deserve each other. And . . . and I HATE feeling like this . . . and . . . and I HATE Sophie for MAKING me feel like this.

Thing On My Mind Number 2: It doesn't feel right to have left without saying goodbye to Sophie. But it serves her right. I may never speak to her again. This thought makes me feel weird and unreal.

Thing On My Mind Number 3: I didn't get to see Rob last night. I sent him a message asking where we should meet – and when – and he sent one back saying that he was really tired and could we make it another time. I TOLD him earlier yesterday that I was going away . . . perhaps he can't face 'goodbyes' – or perhaps he doesn't fancy me any more . . . But he *is* my Fate Mate – isn't he?

'Anything you want to talk about?' Mum asks.

I explain to Mum that my life is unravelling like knitting, and I tell her about not saying goodbye to Rob, or to Sophie, or anyone – apart from the neighbour's cat . . . Mum tells me not to expect too much of Rob as he is very young. Although I don't think I can stop loving Rob, I know that Mum is right. And I say that I should probably go for someone older and more mature . . . Mum swerves the car and says, in an alarmed voice, that that is *not* what she meant at all, and that she would like to see me concentrating on my GCSE work because it is the most important thing at the moment. She sounds stressed again and I realise I have been going on about my own problems and not thinking about how she must be feeling.

'Does it bother you when I go to stay with Dad?' I ask. 'I mean, because of Wendy and the baby.'

Mum sighs. 'To be honest it bothers me a *bit* – but not that much any more . . . It's very kind and thoughtful of you to be concerned, darling, but you don't need to worry about *me*. The most important thing is that your dad really loves you – and you love him – and that's a *good* thing. So I'm glad when you see him.'

'Well . . .' I say, taking a deep breath. 'I'm glad that your colleague is coming to stay.'

'Oh . . . er, are you, darling?' says Mum distractedly. 'That's nice.' We are getting very near to the dropping-off point where we meet Dad.

I am about to ask Mum if it was love at first sight with the colleague – but we have arrived, and there with his arms spread wide in greeting is . . .

'Dad!'

Getting out of Mum's car, I rush to give him a big hug. He hugs me back, says that he likes my red hair, and I feel my troubles retreating to the farthest corner of my mind.

When I arrive, Dad tells me he's going to cook my favourite meal, shepherd's pie. I thank him, and he gives me another big hug. He stayed in and worked – he runs his own computer business from home – while Wendy (his new wife – except that she is not as new as she was) and Alfie and I went to the shop. They live in Eastbury, which is the sort of pretty village you see on picture postcards, all hanging baskets and roses growing round the doors, although the autumn leaves and petals are beginning to fall. I enjoy walking from their small but cosy house to the village shop, pushing Alfie in his pram, while Wendy chats to me and asks me questions about school, boyfriends etc. I realise that she is making an effort to get to know me, but I don't feel like talking about Rob. He hasn't replied to the friendly 'HOW R U?' text which I sent him an hour ago. I tell Wendy that school is boring.

DAD

ALFIE   WENDY

That night, we sit at the dining-room table – laid specially for me, Wendy tells me, pointing out the flowers she bought — to eat our meal, and Alfie sits in his high chair, gurgling and banging a spoon on the tray in front of him. He is *so* cute, but he demands all of Dad's and Wendy's attention. Dad asks me how things are at home but doesn't get to hear my answer as Alfie chooses this moment to throw mashed potato all over the floor. (Dad and Wendy seem very concerned about their new carpet.)

I don't feel part of it. Dad wants us all to watch a DVD after supper — he has got hold of one of my favourites, a romantic comedy called *Lovestruck*, starring gorgeous Brad Rosenthal. But I say that I am really tired, and I just want an early night. Dad looks worried — but Wendy is calling him to help with Alfie.

'I'm OK, Dad — honestly,' I say. 'Just tired.'

At night the house is very quiet — apart from the ticking of the clock on the landing and Alfie's occasional cries — and I can't sleep. The things on my mind are back, trooping round and round in circles, getting nowhere . . . I am horrified that Sophie and I are no longer BMF — and Rob *still* hasn't texted me . . .

Chapter 12
Sophie

TASH LEFT WITHOUT saying goodbye. I don't care. I hate her. How could she say those things about Luke? What if she was right . . .? NO! It's NOT TRUE! I don't think much of Rob, saying nasty things about Luke behind his back – he's not much of a friend. He *is* a bully. Tash has changed LOADS since she met him. I wish she'd go back to how she used to be, before she started repeating what Rob says like a lovesick parrot. I wish things would go back to the way they were before we had boyfriends.

Oh, well. I think Rob and Tash deserve each other – I didn't even WANT to say goodbye to her . . .

Luke loves me – I'm sure he does. So why hasn't he texted me? I sent him an 'LOL XXX' text – that was yesterday, before I went to bed – but I have had nothing back. Now I feel stupid . . . but I'm sure there's a reason why he hasn't replied. Boys aren't good at communicating.

Kyle proved this earlier when I asked him if I could look at the photos of Luke on his phone. He just said: 'Leave me alone!' No explanation! Just: 'Leave me alone!' So I left him alone . . .

I am back in my room listening to Kezia's *Sad Songs* CD, which Tash brought with her and left behind. (I have already listened to *Lament for Lost Souls* by the Melodics six times.) Feeding my heartache with melancholy music and thoughts of the way things were . . . I can hardly see my sketchbook as a thin veil of tears shrouds my eyes. I have just done an unflattering drawing of Rob and Tash, then I turn to the page where I wrote down my resolutions to be a better person. (So long ago. Things were so much simpler then.) And I feel ashamed. But maybe one small chocolate bar won't make much difference now . . .

SCENE FROM SOPHIE'S SKETCHBOOK

There is a knock on the door and Kyle comes into the room.

'Are you OK?' he asks. 'I'm sorry about earlier – I had

things on my mind. But here's my phone — just don't drool over it if you're looking at the pics of Luke.'

Smiling at him bravely through my tears, I say: 'Thanks, Kyle. It's good to see you.'

'Oh God!' Kyle exclaims. 'You're being weird again.' But he comes to sit down beside me. 'What's up?' he asks.

I tell him. He says that 'true love is nothing but pain'. I am not sure that this is very helpful. He explains that Charlotte has dumped him for a boy called Jordan, and that until a short time ago he thought that he would never get over it. But now he feels much better because he is meeting Tom at the skate park, and Tom is more fun to be with than Charlotte because he plays football and likes to have a laugh.

'Charlotte hated football and she didn't laugh much,' Kyle concludes. 'If Luke is making you miserable, perhaps you'd better dump *him* — although it's a shame. I mean, LUKE NORRIS! Wow! But I think you should make it up with Tash — definitely.' I now think that Kyle is *good* at communicating — I wish Luke was.

'I don't know . . .' How could the *Teen Astrologer's Guide to Lurve* have got it *so* wrong? Jupiter is meant to be cavorting in the seventh house of Venus — my life is not *meant* to be a total mess.

Kyle suggests that I walk with him to the skate park, and think about it. I decide that it would probably do me good to get away from the *Sad Songs* for a while, so I agree. Before we leave, I slip my calming stone into my pocket, put on a brave smile (and some Cherrypie and Kiwi lip gloss, just in case) and resolve to think about others in order to take my mind off my own worries.

At the skate park I see a group of girls from my year, and one of them, a girl called Shareen Williams, is in tears. The other girls are trying to comfort her. Now is my chance.

Walking up to Shareen, I put my arm round her shoulders and ask, 'What's wrong?' in a voice packed full of sympathy, empathy and concern for others. I really *do* care. I WANT to help – there is too much sadness in the world.

'The boys were teasing her about her appearance,' one of the other girls explains.

'But they're so wrong!' I exclaim. 'True beauty comes from within and shines out of your eyes.'

Shareen sniffs and looks at me blearily out of reddened, puffy eyes.

'It's true,' I say, calmingly. 'You can't help having a few spots . . .'

'SPOTS?' shrieks Shareen. 'Who said anything about spots? They were teasing me about my hair. Now you've made everything WORSE!' She bursts into loud sobs while her friends tell me to 'Get lost!'

I feel awful. I was only trying to help. Feeling the calming stone cool in my pocket, I walk away. In the distance I can see Kyle kicking a football about with Tom. It makes me smile to see that *someone* is happy. Then I see something that wipes the smile off my face and sends my heart and stomach plummeting like a broken lift down a lift shaft . . .

Luke is with Jasmine – and they are kissing. They obviously think that they can't easily be seen, as they are half hidden by a screen of trees down one side of the playing area – but I have seen enough.

Gulping and choking on my sobs, I half run, half stumble all the way home and back to my room where I collapse on the bed, pouring out my grief into the pillow. There isn't a calming stone in the world powerful enough to assuage *this* sorrow.

So Tash was right. Now she will have the satisfaction of knowing she was right and saying 'I told you so', assuming that she is still talking to me. The Old Tash would not do this – instead she would put her arm round me and comfort me. The New Tash will probably be smugness personified because she and Rob are still an item. She will tell me that 'ROB WAS RIGHT!' I . . . CAN'T . . . BEAR . . . IT!

I can't sleep tonight. The worst thing is that I still *fancy* Luke – but I don't *like* him. Mum knew something was wrong, but I didn't want to talk about it. I sent an angry message to Luke – 'SAW U AND JASMINE 2DAY' – but I have had no reply . . . A disturbing memory of Luke acting the part of Macbeth comes into my mind, together with an uncomfortable image of myself as a pathetic, lovesick Weird Sister, her tongue hanging out as she ogles Macbeth . . . I must draw this in my sketchbook as a warning to myself.

'"*Macbeth does murder sleep . . . the innocent sleep, sleep that knits up the ravelled sleave of care . . . Sophie shall sleep no more . . .*"' My poor, stressed brain rambles on in this manner as I lie, staring at the ceiling . . .

Chapter 13

Natasha

ON TUESDAY I AM woken early by Alfie crying loudly. I hear Dad walking along the landing with him, comforting him. They go downstairs to the kitchen to make Alfie's breakfast – Wendy is obviously having a lie-in.

I wish I didn't feel jealous of Wendy and Alfie (I *love* Alfie – he's sweet), but I can't seem to help it. They demand so much of Dad's attention. I feel as though there isn't room for me, and I feel resentful towards Wendy, and I am TRYING not to hate her – I can't stand it. I can't handle these feelings. I wish I was a nicer person. I find myself thinking of Sophie and her resolutions – this makes me feel worse because it reminds me that Sophie and I are no longer BMF!

'I think you could do with some serious cheering-up – am I right?' Dad enquires gently, as I sit down to breakfast.(Wendy has got up and is feeding toast fingers to Alfie.)

I nod miserably, and hope that I don't start crying into my bowl of Crunchy Pops. I am glad that Dad doesn't press me for the reasons *why* I am upset – I'd rather talk to him when Wendy isn't around.

'How about some retail therapy?' says Wendy, brightly. This is the sort of thing that Sophie would say. 'You don't have too much work on at the moment, do you, darling?' she asks Dad.

'No, no. I can certainly take some time off to take you all into Ditchfield this morning,' Dad replies.

All of us? Couldn't it just be him and me? Apparently not – so I've got a morning in Mothercare buying nappies to look forward to. *Just* want I need – not.

When we get to Ditchfield, and Dad has found a parking space, and Alfie is tucked securely into his buggy, Dad announces his intention of taking Alfie to look at the ducks and swans on the river, while Wendy and I look round the shops and do 'girl stuff' together.

Speechless, I stare at Dad in disbelief – how can he *do* this to me? I came to visit *him* – I can't do 'girl stuff' with Wendy. She's not a 'girl', she's my stepmum. I'm hardly ever on my own with her – Dad's usually there, and now Alfie too. At first, when Dad introduced her to me, I would hardly talk to her. These days I'm polite – but there's a big leap from being 'polite' to doing 'girl stuff together'.

Reluctantly, with several backward glances at Dad's

retreating figure, pushing the buggy, I trail after Wendy, who seems determined to have a good time.

'I know this great shop,' she enthuses. 'It's full of just the sort of clothes that would suit *you* – too young for me, I'm afraid.'

She's not that old – people might mistake us for sisters. I suppose doing 'girl stuff' with Wendy *might* be possible.

Wendy ushers me into a shop called Grip. I have no idea why it is called Grip, but it is full of cool clothes. I am forced to admit to myself that Wendy has good taste. There is even a drop dead gorgeous boy working behind the counter – he has a shock of short dreadlocks and a twinkly smile – he is smiling at me.

'Look at this top, Tash – isn't it great?' says Wendy, holding up a white long-sleeved top with a light blue design.

'Oh, I love it!' I exclaim. Switching my gaze between the boy behind the counter and the cool top, I fail to notice the jutting metal stand of a nearby clothes rail – I trip over it and fall 'splat' onto the ground in front of everyone – including the gorgeous shop assistant.

Having made sure that I am not injured (although I want to cry with embarrassment), Wendy has me on my feet within seconds, hurries me out of the shop and into a café, where she sits me down and tells me to take slow, deep breaths and relax while she gets me a drink.

I am grateful to her – but I bet she gets me a latte. To

my surprise, she returns with two large hot chocolates with cream.

'You've had a shock,' she says. 'You need sugar. I hope you like cream.'

I have just decided that Wendy is very *sensible* – it

'YOU'VE HAD A SHOCK – YOU NEED SUGAR!'

makes perfect sense to increase your sugar intake after a nasty shock, and I am sure that Sophie would agree that any Resolutions to Give Up Chocolate must certainly be put to one side in such a situation.

Thinking about Sophie makes me feel sad and I find myself telling Wendy all about my falling-out with Sophie, and about Rob, and how he hasn't replied to my text. It must be the shock – it's loosened my tongue.

Wendy is very understanding and sympathetic. She says that good friends usually forgive each other – it's just a matter of time. She advises me to stop texting Rob, and to wait for him to text *me*.

When we get back to the car, Dad and Alfie are waiting for us. Dad looks delighted to see that I am looking happy – Wendy doesn't mention my fall . . .

'Oh, no!' she exclaims suddenly, clapping her hand over her mouth. 'I think I left a bag behind in the café – I'll just rush back and get it.'

When she has gone, Dad asks me if I enjoyed myself.

'Yes, Dad. I did.'

'That's good – that's very good.'

Wendy returns with a Grip carrier bag. I don't believe it! She has bought me the cool top. I thank her over and over again.

Then Dad tells me that he and Wendy have something important to ask me – they would like me to be godmother to Alfie. I am speechless. All I know about godmothers is the fairy variety who appear in fairy tales to grant three wishes. But I am delighted to be asked. Dad explains that he has already spoken to Mum about it – he tells me that Mum said that she was happy about it as long as I was happy. I am *very* happy. I now feel like a proper 'part' of Dad's new family. Dad says that both he and Wendy wanted me to be a godparent to Alfie as I would be close to him both in age and family relation-ship, and he would be able to come to me as a friend and big sister. They are also asking Kezia to be a godmother.

I am glad about this as I wouldn't want Kezia to think that I am Dad's favourite, and get jealous.

I feel close to tears when I think of Mum and how it must be hard for her, and how she only thinks of me and not of herself – and this deepens my resolve to make her happy and show her how much I love her. I also feel sad because I would love to tell Sophie my 'news' but we are still not speaking or exchanging texts . . .

Back at the house, I am holding baby Alfie on my lap. I can't believe I'm going to be his godmother. It hasn't really sunk in yet. I really want to tell Sophie . . . Looking down I see that Alfie is smiling up at me. I well up as I smile back . . . I said some horribly hurtful things to Sophie – my Best Mate Forever. But she has probably told Luke what a cow I am, and she may never speak to me again.

Dad comes to sit beside me. He asks me what's wrong, and I tell him. (I find it so easy to talk to him.) He says that things often seem worse than they really are, and he is sure that Sophie and I will make it up with each other. He says that he would feel happier if I spent more time with Sophie and less time with Rob – I think I agree with him – I would feel happier, too. Then he fetches the photograph albums, and we look at photos of when I was younger. There are photos of Mum – this makes me feel sad that she and Dad are no longer

together – but at least Dad hasn't thrown them away. I tell Dad about Mum and the 'male colleague' – Dad looks taken aback, and then he says that he is glad that Mum isn't lonely. I feel happier now that I've told Dad, and he doesn't seem to mind too much. We go on looking through the photo album. There are photos of Sophie and me splashing about in a paddling pool, Sophie and me riding our bikes, Sophie and me . . .

BE-BE-BEEP! I jump violently as my phone vibrates in my pocket – is it a message from Rob? Is it from Sophie?

It is from Kyle. Sophie says that he is always copying numbers from other people's phones so that it looks as though he knows more people. He has obviously copied mine . . . Kyle's message says: 'PLSE TEXT S – SHE WON'T STOP CRYING!'

This sounds like Sophie in Major Crisis Mode! I expect it's something to do with Luke – I wonder what's happened? Has she found out that he's been cheating on her? There must be big trouble in the house of lurve. But I don't know if she'll be pleased to hear from me, after everything I said . . .

I send Sophie a message. It says: 'HI!'

A few minutes later I get a message back.

S2T: HI TASH! I MISS U. U WERE RIGHT BOUT L. I AM SOREEE 4 BAD THINGS I SAID. PLSE CAN WE BE BMF AGAIN?

T2S: YES! C U SOON! MISS U!

BMF (AGAIN!)

A few minutes after I have sent this text, Sophie phones me and tells me EVERYTHING . . . I tell her my news as well, and she is thrilled that I am going to be Alfie's godmother. She tells me that I'll have to remember to send Alfie a card and give him a present on his birthday every year. I tell her that this won't be a problem, especially if she comes with me to help me choose his present – we need to look for a christening gift (the christening will be in the spring). Sophie says that she would *love* to do this.

Chapter 14

Sophie

TASH WILL BE BACK SOON from visiting her dad – I can't wait! I am SOOO pleased that we are BMF again. It is so much easier to cope with the slings and arrows of outrageous fortune (Shakespeare again!) when we are friends. She *didn't* say 'I told you so' when I rang her – she was the old Tash again, saying that she wished she was there to give me a hug, and that she understood how I must be feeling – AWFUL! She also said that she'd rather be BMF with me than have a boyfriend who couldn't be bothered to reply to her texts. She said that she was no longer sure that Rob *was* her Fate Mate . . . but she didn't sound too upset. In fact she sounded really happy – the prospect of becoming Alfie's god-mother seems to have brought back the old Tash.

This morning Tash rang me early to say that she hadn't slept all night and that she'd made up her mind to dump Rob. I told her that I am going to dump Luke

AFTER I have beaten him to a pulp and thrown heavy objects at him. I wouldn't *really* do this – the trouble is, I *still* fancy him! AAARGH!!!

I race round to Tash's house as soon as she texts me to say that she is back. We give each other the BIGGEST HUG! She says that she had a great time at her dad's house, and that he helped her to see things clearly, and that she's looking forward to seeing him again in a fortnight's time – and would I like to go with her next time? She has already asked her dad, and he said it would be fine. I tell her that I would love to.

'But now we need to decide how we're going to dump the boys,' I say, just as Tash's phone beeps. 'Or *if* we're going to,' I continue, hesitating.

'I just got a text from Rob – look!' exclaims Tash. 'He says: "R U back? Can I C U?" So now I'm not sure . . . Wendy was right! I waited for him to text *me* – her advice seems to have worked.'

'And I'll probably want to forgive Luke as soon as I see him,' I say. 'But let's draw up a list of dumping options – just in case.'

Together we draw up a list of dumping options:

1) Dump them by text message, such as:
    i) U R DUMPED!
    ii) U R SOOOOO DUMPED!
   iii) TAKE A RUNNING JUMP – U R DUMPED!!!

2) Dump them face to face. This is less cowardly than dumping them by text. Say something like:
 i) It's not working.
 ii) It's not me – it's you.
 iii) Go out with *you*? Ha ha ha!

3) Say goodbye in a mature and civilised manner, saying that you hope very much that you may be friends in the future, and shake their hand. Walk away with immense dignity.

4) Ignore them. Ignore their calls. Ignore their desperate pleas for forgiveness and a second chance.

At this point we run out of options. Tash's phone beeps again and we bump heads in our eagerness to read the message. It is from Rob (again): 'ME AND L R MATES NOW! WE R AT PARK. WANT TO C US?'

Tash and I exchange glances.

'But you *know* what Luke is like,' Tash says, warningly. 'Luke is a lurve rat!'

'I know – but I'd like to give him the chance to explain himself to me face to face,' I say.

'And kiss you face to face,' Tash teases. I throw a cushion at her.

'I bet that's why *you* want to see Rob,' I retort.

'It might be,' Tash says, smiling. 'And I want to find

out why he didn't reply to my texts. But I want us to be back here in an hour – there's something important I need your help with.'

TURNING OUR BACKS ON BOYS!

Chapter 15

Natasha and Sophie

LOVE HIM OR DUMP HIM? Natasha tells it like it is!

I am so full of glee at the brilliant idea that I have had for Mum's homecoming later that I refuse to tell Sophie what it is, despite her pleas for me to spill my secret!

'Just *wait*!' I say. 'Patience is a virtue – remember your resolutions! We've got other matters to attend to *first*!'

Rob and Luke are at the skate park on their BMXes. Rob waves to me as we approach – he actually stops performing stunts and GETS OFF HIS BIKE to come and say hello – things are looking up. He's never got *off* his bike for me before – I am flattered.

Sophie and Luke have already wandered off on their own, Luke pushing his bike across the grass as they head for the line of trees where Sophie had her nasty shock – perhaps she will have a nice surprise today. I hope so, even though I still feel angry at Luke for hurting my BMF

– but it would be good if all four of us could be friends again. Friends . . . or more?

Rob is telling me how hard he's been training for the Loughborough BMXing championship. This is disappointing – I was hoping he might say:

1) I missed you, Tash!
2) I'm really sorry that I didn't reply to your texts – please forgive me.
3) I love you more than life itself!

I suppose that 3) is too much to hope for – but I'd settle for one of the other two. Perhaps he needs a gentle nudge in the right direction . . .

'Why didn't you reply to my texts?' I ask, interrupting his account of the gruelling keep-fit regime he puts himself through every morning.

'Er – I was busy training,' he replies, weakly.

I feel irritated by this reply, so I ask another provocative question. I am hoping to provoke some sort of emotion – I *know* that Rob has strong feelings about things after I was on the receiving end of his outburst about Luke's behaviour.

'What about Luke?' I ask. 'You seem to have forgiven him pretty easily, considering you were so angry.'

Rob looks thoughtful. 'He was really, really sorry,' he says. 'He was gutted when he realised that Sophie had caught him with Jasmine – I think she sent him a text or something. He's not all bad – he doesn't *want* to hurt anyone – he just can't resist . . . er . . . girls. Oh – and he's putting in a lot more practice on his bike now.'

'What about you?' I ask, interrupting him again. 'Can you resist girls?' Provocative – or what?!

'Yes,' Rob replies.

This is the WRONG answer – I *wanted* him to say: 'Yes – but I can't resist *you*!'

I can tell that he is about to get on his bike again. I want him to say SOMETHING about US! Is there an 'us'?

'Do you like me?' I ask. Desperate rather than provocative.

'Yes, of course. And you've got the most kissable mouth . . .' He leans across his bike and kisses me . . . my legs buckle and I have to lean on the bike as well. After several delicious minutes (during which I have lost control of my legs completely), he stops kissing me and straightens up, smiling. Unfortunately, he lets go of the bike – as I have jelly legs I lose my balance and fall forwards (SPLAT! AGAIN!!!) on top of the bike . . . I land awkwardly, sprawled over the main frame of the bike, one of the stunt pegs hitting my shoulder painfully as I fall. I can hear people laughing . . .

'You idiot!' shouts Rob. 'What have you done to my bike – it's going to be scratched to bits down one side and – look – YOU'VE BENT A SPOKE!'

My shoulder hurts, and my face is burning with the humiliation of falling over *again* in public – but I am vaguely aware that Rob is a TOTAL PIG who only cares about his stupid bike and doesn't give a damn about ME or the pain I'm in – and I NEVER EVER want to see him again!!! EVER!!! I tell him this.

A few other people, realising that I am hurt, have come over to ask if I'm OK, while Rob, having moved me out of the way (I felt that he was moving me out of the way so that he could get a closer look at his bike), crouches down to examine the bent spoke . . .

'Are you OK?' Rob asks, at last. But it is too late – the damage is done. I don't even bother to reply . . . A tear slides down my cheek.

Then I see Sophie – she is running across the grass towards me! I can't see Luke . . .

LOVE HIM OR DUMP HIM? Sophie tells it like it is!

Tash *refuses* to tell me what is so important that she needs my help with it later. I try to wear her down with questions (this usually works) – but she won't spill.

Then I see Luke – and everything else goes out of my mind. My heart does front and back flips, and my stomach goes into spin cycle. I suppose I still fancy him . . .

On the way to the skate park – when I wasn't trying to squeeze Tash's secret out of her – I was planning how I would behave when I saw Luke. I decided that I should be cool, bearing my emotional pain with dignity – so that he would end up feeling like a complete WORM! And then I would forgive him, providing that he was truly sorry and promised *never* to behave so heartlessly again . . .

'Oh, er – hi, Luke!' I feel myself blushing bright red.

Luke is blushing, too. 'Er – hi!' he says, giving me that wonderful inside-melting lopsided smile.

'Would you . . . like to go for a walk?' I ask, hesitantly. I wonder whether I should say something about 'unfinished business' – but I decide against it . . . I *don't* want to sound like Jasmine, whom I now LOATHE and DESPISE!!!

'Er . . .' says Luke, pushing his bike along beside me. 'Um. How are you?'

I want to say: 'I am bearing the pain you inflicted on me with dignity.' Instead, I say, 'Fine. You?'

'Fine.'

We are heading for *those* trees where I saw him kissing Jasmine. I feel sick . . .

'Look, I didn't mean to hurt you,' says Luke, suddenly. 'I'm so sorry – really I am. You didn't deserve that.'

'Oh! Er . . .'

'Can I kiss you?'

'MMRRFF!!!' I was about to say 'Maybe!' in order to play it cool and keep him hanging on – but his tongue is already touching my tonsils.

He stops kissing me and gives me a friendly pat on the shoulder.

'Friends?' he says, confusingly. My 'friends' don't normally stick their tongues down my throat.

'Er . . . sure,' I reply, horribly aware that the Smile From Hell is attempting to make a comeback. It is because I am feeling anxious – I don't seem to have got the hang of kissing – or is it Luke's fault? And I don't know whether Luke wants to be JGF or MTJGF! I *think* he really likes me . . . I *think* he really *is* sorry.

We carry on walking around the park, passing the children's play area where some girls of my own age are sitting on swings, chatting.

I think I had better get the situation straight with Luke, so, frowning down at the grass in concentration, I begin to say what is on my mind: 'Luke, I really like you – I want you to know that. And I *want* things to be right between us – more than anything. But you really hurt me. Do you understand? I can't risk that sort of hurt again . . . so I've got to be sure . . . that you're not going to . . . to . . .'

Looking up, I realise that Luke is looking at the group of girls, who are all simpering and waving at him. One of them rushes up to him and gives him a hug. He hugs her back, and then she runs back to her friends, giggling.

'You haven't been listening to a word I've said, have you?' I exclaim, in exasperation.

'Er . . . what?' Luke asks, looking confused.

'Exactly! If you want to be with me, you've got to change.'

'I can't. I'm always going to be me. It would be nice if you liked me the way I am. I'm not *that* bad, am I? And you like kissing.'

'Er . . .'

Luke's phone beeps.

'Don't tell me – it's your mum,' I say in a mildly sarcastic tone. Things aren't working out the way I hoped they would . . .

'No,' Luke replies, apparently unaware that I am being sarcastic. 'It's Jasmine. She wants to know if I'm going to her party.'

'Oh. And *are* you?' I say, through gritted teeth.

'Um . . .'

Oh, I don't believe it! He can't make up his mind. If he really cared about me, he'd have nothing to do with Jasmine. I am suddenly aware that I don't fancy him quite as much as I did even a short while ago. He is too – what is the word I'm looking for? – too *immature*.

'I don't think this is working,' I say, quietly.

'What?' says Luke, looking puzzled.

'It's not working between us.'

'What isn't?'

'I mean – this relationship isn't going anywhere. It's not working for me.'

'Er . . . are you dumping me?'

'I . . . I think so.'

'Oh, but I really like you.'

AAARGH! I MUST NOT WEAKEN! I'll only get hurt again. I remember Dumping Option Number 4: 'Ignore their desperate pleas for forgiveness and a second chance!'

Taking a deep breath I say: 'I'm sorry, Luke – it's over.'

'OK.'

OK??! He was meant to fall to his knees and beg me to take him back!!!

Trying not to look too disappointed, I turn and walk away. My eyes fill with tears – but at the same time I feel proud of myself for doing something so difficult. I have just *dumped* Luke Norris. LUKE NORRIS!!! One of the most yearned-for boys in the whole . . . ohmigod. . . what have I DONE?!

I hesitate, wondering whether to run back to him and say I made a mistake. Then I see that he is sitting on a swing with the girl who hugged him on his lap – so he obviously didn't waste any time replacing me! Now I KNOW I made the right decision. I have a sudden urge to rush over and push him off the swing, girl and all. But something distracts me . . .

A slight crashing sound from the skate park causes me to look round and I see . . . Tash. She is lying on the ground, on top of Rob's bike. She must have been riding the bike, and had a fall – why isn't Rob helping her up? I can hear him shouting – he sounds angry. What *is* going on?

I start running in Tash's direction – I think she needs me. I sometimes have a sixth sense for when people – particularly Tash – need me, but I've been so obsessed with Luke recently that my Sixth Sense packed up and left, along with my common sense.

Tash looks really miserable when I reach her – she is crying! She tells me that her shoulder hurts, but I have a feeling that Rob has upset her, too. She won't even look at him – he is looking sheepish, hovering nearby with his bike.

'Er – will you be OK?' he asks. 'I'm sorry I shouted.'

Tash doesn't say anything.

'I'll . . . I'll take her home,' I say. 'Come on, Tash, honey – put your arm around my shoulder, if you can . . .'

'It's OK – I'm feeling better now you're here,' says Tash, quietly.

I don't like seeing my BMF so upset – it has put my own problems right to the back of my mind – all I care about is getting Tash home and making sure she's OK. At last I feel that I am really keeping my Resolution to Be Nice to Parents, Siblings, Tash and Teachers.

On the way back to her house Tash tells me what happened. I tell her that she was quite right to dump

Rob. How *could* he treat my BMF like that? I tell her that I dumped Luke – Tash seems relieved, but asks if I'm OK.

'I'm OK now I'm with you,' I say, truthfully.

'Same here,' Tash agrees.

We link arms – Tash says her shoulder feels slightly sore but that it has stopped aching.

'Let's think about something else for a while,' I suggest. 'I promise not to mention Luke for at least half an hour – if you'll do the same with Rob.'

Tash nods agreement. 'Fine by me,' she says.

'Good! So, fill me in on this idea you've had – something to do with your mum?' I ask.

'Ohmigod!' Tash exclaims. 'We haven't got long.'

She explains that she wants to prepare a romantic dinner for two for her mum and a male colleague whom her mum is bringing home this evening.

'She's never brought a man home before,' says Tash. 'And he's staying the night. I'm pretty sure it must be serious – she's been saying things recently about meeting the Right Man. I think she was trying to get me used to the idea before she introduced him. And I thought she was a Lonely Heart!' I am nervous about meeting the Male Colleague, but I must learn to trust Mum's taste in men (she married Dad, after all).

'Wow! How do you feel about your mum with another man?'

'Strange. But then I talked to Dad, and he said he thought it was a good thing if Mum wasn't lonely any more – and I felt better after I talked to him. And Mum's been brilliant about letting me be a godmother, and all that – so I really want to do something special for her – to show I love her . . .'

'That's beautiful, Tash!' I exclaim. 'I'd love to help!'

Kezia's reaction to Tash's romantic dinner for two idea is not quite so encouraging. She gives a whoop of laughter and spills her coffee. Then she sees the look on Tash's face, and apologises.

'I'm serious, Kez,' says Tash. 'My visit to Dad's really helped me to see things clearly. I've realised that Wendy isn't a wicked stepmother – in fact, she was really kind to me. She and Dad are really happy and they want us to be happy too, that's why they've asked us to be godmothers.'

'I know – isn't it great?' says Kezia, beaming.

'Yes, so why shouldn't Mum have a chance of happiness and romance in her life?'

'I understand what you're saying, Tash,' says Kezia. 'But you can't just wish happiness on other people, no matter how much you may want to. This colleague may just be a friend.'

'If I'm wrong, I'm wrong,' says Tash. 'But I don't think I am. And I *do* want to do something special for Mum.

The only thing that bothers me is that I don't want anyone to take Dad's place.'

'No one ever can,' says Kezia, gently. 'Whatever happens. Is your shoulder OK? You keep rubbing it.'

We tell Kezia about Rob and Luke, and she says that they sound very immature. I agree. Go, Kez! She insists on examining Tash's shoulder and rubbing Deep Heat ointment onto it. 'Just bruised, I think,' she remarks.

Tash is getting twitchy. 'We really need to get on with the Romantic Meal for Two!' she urges. 'We need to get cooking. My shoulder's fine – honestly!'

Kezia wants to know where the rest of us are going to be while Tash's mum and the Male Colleague are enjoying their romantic meal for two.

'We'll be in the kitchen,' says Tash, firmly. 'Preparing the food and serving it. We'll tell them we ate earlier – you can't have a romantic meal for six or seven.'

'OK – so what are you going to give them to eat?' Kezia asks.

Tash looks in the fridge – there are two eggs and a half-empty tin of baked beans.

'I hardly think that one egg and about ten baked beans each are going to put them in the mood,' Kezia remarks, trying not to laugh. Then, seeing the despairing look on Tash's face, I suggest that we go back to my house and look through Mum's cookery books.

'Great idea!' Tash exclaims. 'We've got about two hours till Mum gets back.'

'I hope Mum has a *Quick Romantic Meals for Two* book,' I say.

After poring over Mum's cookery books for nearly quarter of an hour, our mouths are watering but we have not made up our minds.

Then Dad appears with an enormous marrow left over from the ones he grew earlier in the year, and Mum suggests that we stuff it. It is Wednesday, so Mum is home early from the library.

'That doesn't sound very romantic,' I remark.

AN ENORMOUS MARROW 'Stuffed marrow is very nice,' Mum insists. 'It's called mock duck.'

Tash and I stare at her as if she is mad – the marrow looks nothing like a duck.

Mum produces the other ingredients that we will need, including sage and onion stuffing, and tells us how to prepare it.

'I suppose it *could* be OK,' I whisper to Tash, who nods doubtfully.

Dad, who is also on half-term, gives us some apples to make into an apple pie – and, after Mum has whispered to him audibly that we are preparing a romantic meal for Tash's mum, Tash looks thoroughly embarrassed. He gives us a bunch of late chrysanthemums from the garden to make a table centrepiece.

With a pang of conscience I realise that I haven't been very nice to Dad – telling him to stay in the car, as if I am ashamed of him, and then worrying him by being late meeting him after my date with Luke, not to mention arguing and whingeing . . . it is about time I worked harder at my Resolution to Be Nice to Parents, Siblings and Teachers.

'I . . . I like your cardigan, Dad,' I say.

'Oh – er . . . thank you,' says Dad, looking disconcerted, but pleased!

Back at Tash's house, we get on with the preparations. The marrow is so huge that we cut it in half, and decide to stuff half of it with mince and half of it with sage and onion – the vegetarian option, which I prefer (I am *almost* a vegetarian). It is very messy to prepare, and Tash and I get the giggles. I am so glad that life is back to 'normal', although I can't help thinking about Luke . . . then I feel proud of myself for standing up to him instead of letting him mess me around. At least my pride is intact, if not my heart. My heart is in a zillion pieces. My great romance was *sooo* short-lived . . .

'SOPHIE!' Tash calls me. 'Come down to earth, will

you? I need your help. This mock-duck-thing is fighting back.'

Together we wrap it in silver foil, as Mum suggested, and put it in the oven.

'Now for the apple pie!' Tash exclaims.

'We could call it a Love Apple Pie,' I suggest. Gemini inspiration strikes again.

'A love apple is another name for a pomegranate,' says Kezia, walking into the kitchen and inspecting the mess.

'Pomegranate pie,' I exclaim.

'Whatever,' says Tash. 'We really need to get on with it . . .'

'I hope you're going to clear up all this mess,' Kezia remarks, helpfully.

I am kept busy rushing between both our houses, fetching pastry ingredients, cream for the Love Apple Pie (Mum gives me some money to buy some from the Minimart), some romantic background music (I grab Kezia's *Sad Songs* and *Lament for Lost Souls* CDs – I hope

they don't make me cry as they both remind me of Luke). I also grab some candles (this is not a problem as Mum and I both love candles, and we have loads). It is already getting dark outside.

* * *

'I'm really nervous,' says Tash. 'I hope Mum's going to be pleased. We've cleared up *most* of the mess . . .'

'She's going to love it,' I say, reassuringly. 'The mock-duck-thing smells delicious, and the Love Apple Pie is only *slightly* burnt, and you won't notice the burnt bits when you cover them with cream . . .'

There is a towering heap of whipped cream in a small bowl – I think I may have prepared too much.

'Mum should be back any minute,' says Tash. 'It's about ten minutes since she phoned, isn't it? Would you light the candles? My hands are shaking. Do you think I'm mad, Sofe?'

'What kind of question is that? No, I don't. You're just giving your mum a really nice treat, and there's nothing wrong with that . . .'

Tash and Kezia greet their mum with big hugs.

'Roderick's fetching the luggage from the car,' she says. Roderick must be the male colleague.

'I could have a stepdad called Roderick,' Tash whispers to me.

'Ssh!' I hiss.

Tash ushers her mum into the living room (the living room and dining area are joined together into one big room), where we have cleared most of the furniture to the sides of the room, leaving a small table (a plastic one from the patio furniture in the garden), covered in a white tablecloth, and two chairs in the middle of the room.

'What the . . . I mean . . . what lovely flowers,' Tash's mum exclaims. 'And what a lot of candles. What's this all about?'

'It's for you, Mum,' says Tash. 'And . . . er . . . Roderick.'

'What about everyone else?' Tash's mum asks, looking disconcerted.

'We ate earlier,' Tash says. No, we didn't – my stomach is rumbling and the smell of the mock-duck-thing is making my mouth water . . .

Kezia is leaning her head on her mum's shoulder, giggling.

I turn up the volume on the CD player – I have put on *Sad Songs* – and the theme from *Titanic* swells as Roderick walks in the room . . .

He is short, fat and balding, and wears thick-lensed glasses with black frames. He looks confused . . .

RODERICK

I realise that Tash's mum and Kezia are *both* giggling. Soon, they are helpless with laughter and have to collapse onto a nearby sofa. Roderick, looking dazed – he has just realised, too late, that he has walked into a Madhouse – joins in the laughter.

When Tash's mum has recovered, she thanks Tash

and me for the best homecoming ever – and explains that she doesn't think that she and Roderick can consume a whole stuffed marrow between them, not to mention an enormous apple pie and mountains of whipped cream. We don't take too much persuading to help them eat the romantic meal for two, sitting with plates on our laps on the chairs round the room. (The mock-duck-thing is delicious, although the marrow is crunchy.) Tash's mum and Roderick, sitting at the beautifully laid table in the middle of the room, have second helpings of Love Apple Pie and raise a toast to us all, especially to Tash, who can't stop smiling . . .

LOVE APPLE PIE

'It was all worth it,' says Tash, as we chill out in her room after the meal is over (her mum and Roderick have excused us from washing up). 'It was worth it just to see Mum laugh like that. It must have done her good because she said she was sorry to me just now for being such a bad-tempered so-and-so, and that she'd rather spend more time with me and Kez than with anyone else – and she's going to try and cut down on her work-load, so we can do more mother and daughter stuff together – like shopping. But I hope she doesn't want me to drink latte . . . And I told her all about my visit to Dad's – we've never really discussed my visits before. I feel better now that I can tell Mum about it. She really likes the top that Wendy bought me – and she says she thinks that I'll make the *best* godmother and Wendy and Dad made a wise choice in asking Kez and me.'

'That's great, Tash,' I say. 'So it doesn't matter that Roderick's happily married.'

'No, I don't think he was Mum's type, anyway. Did you see how relieved he looked when Geoffrey arrived. Another man to rescue him – he probably thought that we were going to kidnap him and keep him as a sex slave.'

'YEUK! GROSS!'

'Sorry,' Tash apologises – and then we both get serious giggles.

'So, are you over Luke?' Tash asks, recovering her breath.

'No, but I'm getting there,' I reply, trying to sound more in control of the situation – and in control of my life – than I really feel . . . *Why* did Luke have to turn out to be such a heart-mangler? I reeeally liked him . . . and I think he liked me . . . but he didn't have a clue how to handle a real boyfriend/girlfriend relationship – he just wanted to handle GIRLS! 'I'm going to focus on my resolutions,' I say. 'And practise Zen breathing. I don't think Luke was a Leo after all – he is probably a water sign – a bit wet. He didn't have the guts to tell me what was going on – he just saw Jasmine behind my back.'

'True. And you're right about the star sign stuff – I

asked Rob what star signs he and Luke were, because I knew you wanted to know – it turns out they're *both* Pisces.'

'Oh, wow! Fish on bicycles!' I exclaim.

Tash give me a look – then we both burst out laughing.

'Relationships between Gemini and Pisces are always difficult,' I remark. 'But the worst thing was that Luke's behaviour led to US falling out. How did *that* happen?'

PISCES AND GEMINI = 🙁

Tash shrugs and pulls a face. 'I don't want to think about it,' she says. 'I'm just glad it's all over.'

'I agree – relationships between Pisces and Sagittarius aren't too good, either. You and Rob have proved *that*.'

PISCES AND SAGITTARIUS = 🙁

Tash sighs and looks wistful. 'He *did* have THE BEST BUM, though,' she says.

'Tash, *honestly!*'

We laugh even more. 'I'm so glad we're BMF again,' I exclaim.

'Me too,' says Tash, putting her arm round my shoulders. 'Gemini and Sagittarius are mega compatible, as you're always telling me.' She smiles – I smile too.

'I think that being BMF is better than having boyfriends – it's less complicated,' I say.

'Yes, and I didn't like the way that having boyfriends brought out the worst in us – I kept being angry, and jealous, and selfish and stupid – vice on legs!' Tash agrees.

'You weren't *that* bad!' I exclaim. 'I wasn't exactly virtue personified myself – I think I broke *all* my resolutions. At least we proved that we're human – a strange bundle of vices *and* virtues. Would you like some chocolate?'

'Yes – my spot's nearly gone. So, are we going to Lucy Lightfoot's Hallowe'en Party on Friday?'

'Definitely! I thought we could go as . . .'

'The Weird Sisters!' Tash exclaims.

'That should guarantee that the boys steer *well* clear of us,' I remark.

'I don't mind – I don't think I'm ready to meet my Fate Mate just yet,' says Tash. 'Let's forget about MTJGF and all that, for the time being. Let's stay – BMF!'